PIRATES' GOLD

PIRATES' GOLD

H. BEDFORD-JONES

WILDSIDE PRESS

PIRATES' GOLD

Originally published in *Adventure* magazine,
December 20, 1922.

This edition published in 2008 by Wildside Press, LLC.
www.wildsidebooks.com

CHAPTER 1

It was past six bells and growing on to noon, and I was a homesick man as I stood on the quay below London Bridge and watched the *King Sagamore* swinging on her hawser out in the tideway. For she was Virginia-owned, and I, George Roberts of Virginia, knew her well, so that the sight of her was like a touch of home to me.

Also, I had a vile headache, and my memory of the previous night's events was very hazy. I had met a number of other captains, and I think some ship-owners, at the Royal Arms, though I could remember only Ned Low and the dark man, Russel, because I liked the one and disliked the other. I seemed to remember that Low had promised his interest to try to get me a ship, or else a chief mate's berth, but I could recall little of what he had said, except that he told some gorgeous yarns of the Guinea trade.

"Good morning, Captain Roberts!" came a voice, and I turned to see Russel himself approaching.

I greeted him without pleasure, for there was a sneer in his eyes, and I did not like his gold-laced hat and jeweled fingers, or the look in his dark face.

"You seem mighty busy," he went on, his heavy-lidded gaze searching me. "The cap'n put you under the table, I hear! Well, what think you of the *King Sagamore?*"

"Out of trim," I responded. "She's down by the head, or I'm a Dutchman!"

"Oh!" said Russel, eying me. "But you're a Virginian, sir — and a seaman to boot! I never heard of seamen coming from Virginia or the other colonies."

This angered me, as it also puzzled me. Why on earth the man should want to pick a quarrel, I could not see.

But, knocking out my pipe and smiling, I obliged him swiftly.

"Plenty you never heard of, I imagine! Particularly here in England."

"Eh?"

He bent his black brows upon me, scowling.

"How mean you?" he added.

"Why, just this: What was your name before you made it Russel?"

At that, his white teeth showed. He clapped hand to belt as if feeling for a pistol, and I laughed at him.

"Aye, try it with a Virginian!" I told him and chuckled again. "Think you're on the high seas, my bucko? Russel, forsooth! If you're not a Portugee, I don't know my business! Aye, snarl all you please — and ladies' rings to your fingers. You cursed fool, don't you know they hang pirates in London town? How long since you were on the Account, as the gentry of that profession term it?"

That reached him between wind and water, as it were. I really meant to taunt him into action, since I wanted to feel my fist in his dark face; but I went too far. His hands dropped. He stood motionless, his eyes eating into me, and they become bloodshot.

"On the Account!" he repeated the phrase, a thickness in his voice. "You speak glibly of it! Perhaps you've been on the Account yourself, my fine Virginia sailor?"

"Why, perhaps I have," said I cheerfully. "And what of it?"

He looked at me for another moment, then turned on his heel and strode away very swiftly, as one who goes of set purpose. I looked after him, frowning. He had been at the tavern with Captain Low the previous night. Ned Low was an engaging rascal of the sort that men love, had been master of a Guineaman, and had traded at the Indies. Russel was of a very different stripe; a sinister man, certainly no Englishman, and I wondered that Ned Low would keep company with him.

However, I dismissed the matter, filled my pipe afresh and turned to watch the ship out in the stream. She was making ready to sail, and to a seaman's eye she presented some uncommonly interesting aspects.

That homesick feeling grew on me as I looked. My first voyage had been made in her, under old Andrew Scott — a cold and hard master he was, too! Anyone who had sailed with Scott had tales to brag of. But Cap'n Scott was dead and gone these two years, thanks to a drinking bout with Sandy Fisher aboard the *Margaret* at Barbados; for Sandy craftily mixed some rare claret in the rum, and Cap'n Scott never rose from under the table.

Well, Scott was dead, and here was I a captain, and yonder the old *King Sagamore*! Heartily did I wish that I were commanding her or at least aboard of her, since I was down to my last guinea, with no hope of a ship except I took out a slaver, for which I had no stomach.

Gossip along the quay told me that she was bound for Virginia, but I doubted this. She was in ballast, and no ship went to Virginia in ballast these days. Also she had bent a new suit of canvas and was fresh-varnished; and I, knowing how stingy were her owners, realized that this was something like a miracle.

What was more, I perceived a featherbed being put aboard her from the lighter alongside. A featherbed, indeed! No wonder all the Thames boatmen jeered her as they passed, and the crew of a fishing-lugger tied at the quay began to bawl comments which set the river in a roar of laughter. I wondered who was going to use that featherbed.

One cannot deny that the *King Sagamore* has a certain roll to her in the best of seas; an uneasy and fretful roll, as if endeavoring to shake loose of the bloodstains that have sunk into her teak. Even old Cap'n Scott had groaned and left the deck at times.

Just now I heard a voice calling out:

"There 'e be, sir! That's 'im a-smoking of the 'bacca!"

I glanced about, to see a quay loafer pointing me out to a gentleman approaching rapidly. I faced about to meet this stranger in some surprise.

He was a man in a hurry; a small fellow of forty-odd, wizened and thin in the cheeks, his eyes very sparkling. From his heaving chest and awry wig, he had lately been running. As he strode up to me he produced a snuffbox with a great air of grandeur.

"Your pardon, sir," he addressed me, his words rapid and with authority. "You are Captain Roberts, the Virginian?"

"I am," was my response.

"My name is Dennis Langton, merchant and goldsmith, living at the Wheatsheaf in Lombard Street. I had word this morning from Low that you'd be sailing with us."

He rattled this all out in a breath. Then he flung a glance over his shoulder and suddenly thrust the snuffbox at me.

"Here, take this and fetch it aboard wi' you — move sharp now! Tell Ned that I'll come aboard as he drops downstream. Give it to him and no other. With you this side Gravesend — Devil sink me! The dogs have caught the trail — hide it, lad —"

Leaving the snuffbox hidden in my fist, the spry little man darted away from me and ran for cover like a hunted rabbit. I gaped after him, thinking him a madman until the burst of shouts went up from the running men.

"Stop thief!" went up the yells, shrill and sharp with the hunting fever. "Escape! Trip him up — 'scape! 'Prentices out — stop thief — king's name! Pirate and thief —"

Upon and past me swept a shrilling throng in a mad rush, two constables in the lead. Langton vanished in among the buildings, and they after him, and the chorus of yells was swiftly drowned in the noise of the city.

I stood there staring after the rout, until the whimsicality of it all drew a laugh from me. The swift change from the pompous manner and address to the wild flight was ludicrous. The incident was strange and unreal — a merchant of Lombard Street pursued as thief and pirate!

Pirate! Dennis Langton! Suddenly the name flashed across my consciousness and startled me. Three years previously, or rather four, since it was early in 1720, I was mate aboard the ship *Susannah*, owned by a merchant of Southwark Side, near London. There had been much talk aboard her of how she had fallen prey to a brace of pirates near Madeira last voyage and had later escaped. Spriggs was one of the rovers, the same who was lately hanged at Tyburn and still hangs there.

And the other one — Now the name came back to me clear enough! Langton, and none other; Dennis Langton, a soft-spoken man, who was reputed to have murdered many with his own hand.

Could the pirate Langton be the same man as this merchant and goldsmith? Most unlikely, and yet all things are possible in this world!

Now came suspicion that he had stolen the snuffbox which he forced on me, and that I might be taken for a thief. This vanished when I opened my hand. The box was a small one of black wood, absolutely worthless. Nor had the little man the look of a cut-purse.

And what was it he had said about Captain Low? A message for Low, too. And what was that about my shipping with Low? I felt bewildered.

Thrusting the snuffbox into my pocket, I drew again on my pipe, frowning over this singular incident. I was still turning it over in my mind perplexedly, when there arose a new and more singular matter which drove it completely out of my head; and no wonder!

Hearing my name called, I looked around to see Captain Low himself coming toward me, bravely puffing at a pipe and laughing to himself over some inward joke.

"Ha, Roberts! A fine morning to you, George! Damn me, but we had a pretty rouse last night! Why are you standing thus idle in the market place?"

"Why, for lack of work!"

Smiling, I gave him a grip of the hand.

"It seems to me that you said something about looking you up today — but I confess that last rum punch we brewed put a stopper on my brain! Sink me if I can remember a thing."

"What!"

Low gave me a singular yet whimsical look.

"Come, lad! You don't mean to say that you can't remember our discussion?"

"Not a thing," I said ruefully. "I've lost even the name of your ship, Ned!"

He broke into a roar of laughter, dropped his pipe and smashed it, roared again, then clapped me heartily on the shoulder and swung me about.

"There she lies, Roberts, damn me, this is a creamy jest! Wow! Wait until I tell John Russel about this! And you entered with me as chief mate, too! Oh, lad, ha' pity on me! Yonder's the *King Sagamore* with poor Gunner Basil loading the last aboard; and me sleeping abed all morning thinking you stood on her deck!"

"Good Lord!" I stammered. "D'you mean to say that I, George Roberts, shipped as chief mate with you —"

He fell to roaring again with laughter, and I chimed in, helpless to withstand it. We stood there like two fools, holding our sides and sending up shouts of mirth that drew curious folk about to stare and wonder if we were loose from Bedlam.

At length I came out of the fit of laughter, and we walked apart down the quay, discussing matters. When I told Low how I had been homesick for the *King Sagamore*, he began to bellow again.

His news struck me with incredulity, but a glad man I was for the carouse of the night before, since I appeared to have landed a good berth with a man I liked. Ned Low was fully as tall as I, and even wider in the shoulder; a lean man, his face brown and hard as if carven from mahogany, but ever ready to slip into the cheeriest laughter man ever heard. He had a whimsical touch about him, and I think had run away from Oxford for love of the sea, since he could quote the classics by the hour and spoke sometimes of Magdalen Towers.

Well, he speedily made it clear to me that I was signed with him, and that he had all morning supposed me to be aboard, at which we laughed again.

"Russel came back and dragged me from table just as I was sitting down to breakfast with word that you were standing on the quay like a man in a dream," he concluded with a final chuckle. "So I came along to see —"

"Russel!" I said, and frowned. "Does he sail with us?"

"Aye."

Low took my arm frankly and turned me eye to eye with him.

"Listen, Roberts! We've scant time to talk — I must get aboard and see to things. But you're a man after my own heart; I drank you under the table last night to make certain, since rum brings out the worst of a man!

"I know you and Russel must fall out. That's as it should be; but look out that Russel doesn't slip a knife into you. Understand? I have to take him as second mate, willy-nilly, and as we explained last night — Well, run along and get your things, and don't miss the tide on your life! I must aboard."

He turned, calling to a wherry just leaving the landing-stairs and made her with a swift run and a leap. I marveled at his catlike agility, responded to his wave of the hand, and turned to seek my own clothes at the Hare and Hounds, fortunately close by.

For all that I was a happy-go-lucky young devil this morning's affair left me in somewhat of a daze. Or perhaps the rum punch contributed to that effect. However, I was gradually coming to an understanding of things. Russel had come up to me in an evil humor, thinking that I was shirking my duty by loafing ashore; which would well account for his attitude.

Not until I had nearly reached my lodgings did I recall that extraordinary meeting with the man Dennis Langton, and clapped hand to pocket with an exclamation. I had clear forgotten to speak of him to Ned Low!

However, no matter now. It was evident that he must have seen Low that morning, or have heard from him that I was in charge of the ship.

I packed my trunk and stepped in to the ordinary to pay off my landlord. Just then a number of men came crowding in with much high talk, amid which I caught the name of Langton. At that I turned and listened, while the landlord gaped likewise.

"And to think that Langton has all this while been a merchant in Lombard Street!" cried one man with a volley of oaths. "A pretty pass we're coming to in London town!"

"They say," chimed in another, "that he has already sold out his business and was in shape to skip the city —"

"All by accident he was betrayed," spoke up another, a late comer. "You've not heard? Zounds, a ripping story! In Lombard Street itself, only this morning, gentlemen! He came face to face with a shipman whom he'd plundered years ago, was recognized, dodged the hue and cry and broke clear away. Now the constables are searching the city for him, and the waterside as well. A pirate at loose — zounds!"

I paid my score, engaged a man to carry down the trunk and went my way somewhat thoughtfully.

This Dennis Langton, known for a pirate, was a friend of Low and was hoping to get aboard the *King Sagamore*. I was going as mate aboard that ship. So was John Russel; and my words had stung Russel that morning. Russel like Langton, had been on the Account, as those who take to piracy term the profession.

What about Ned Low? He was one of them; no use shirking the fact. This fine Virginia ship was going a-sailing on a mighty queer cruise, in ballast at that!

And what about me, George Roberts of Virginia?

Why, that was simple enough! Duty lay clear and straight before me — inform the authorities, have everyone aboard the *King Sagamore* laid by the heels, and become a popular hero! The ship would be saved to its owners and everybody happy.

Against this there balanced Ned Low's frank and keen blue eyes, the clap of his hand on my shoulder, the comradely liking I bore him. Aye, because I liked him I laughed at duty! Besides I was never a great hand at informing. If I want a thing done, I go do it; this running to catch-polls and constables is not to my mind.

So we came down again to the quay, and as I pocketed my pipe my hand touched the black snuffbox. I drew out the thing and looked at it, pressed the catch and opened it. Inside there was no snuff, but a folded, bone-hard bit of vellum. I put the thing away once more.

"Let sleeping dogs lie!" I reflected. "Dennis Langton may be caught. If he's been posing as a merchant here in London, he'll be well known and should be caught in an hour's time. That may simplify matters a bit.

"As for Ned Low, I trust him more than a little, and he should have sense enough to know that I'm not going on the Account. Perhaps that's not his own intention, either! I may be wronging him."

I called a wherry and was taken out toward the ship. As we approached her I fell to laughing again; for I had not the least notion whither she was bound or on what errand. And I remembered that featherbed going aboard, so that the whole affair struck me afresh with such whimsical humor that I could not refrain from laughing. Captain Low looked over the rail as we drew near, and he caught the infection and began to roar again with mirth, and was still grinning as I came over the side.

"Welcome!" he cried, and struck hands again, a hearty grip. "What's so merry?"

"Why, I can't remember where we are bound for," I said. "Guinea or the plantations?"

"It wasn't mentioned," and Low chuckled. "The Verde Islands, if you want to know, and then Barbados or elsewhere."

"Then we stow salt at the islands, do we?"

Low glanced around, saw that we were alone and gave me a straight look.

"Nay, Roberts — we stow gold! Art satisfied? And not on the Account neither."

I nodded, and once again forgot about Dennis Langton's message.

CHAPTER 11

After stowing my duffel away in one of the stern cabins I came on deck again and inspected things. Captain Low had everything shipshape, and now there was little to do save to await the tide. Russel had not come aboard as yet, either.

Truly a sweet ship was the *King Sagamore*! Built originally for the India trade, she had much of the black teak in her making, and this was ever kept oiled and waxed, in neat contrast to her white deck and varnished spars and the new canvas stowed aloft. At her bow the torso of a feathered savage was set for figurehead; glass eyes the Sagamore had in his painted visage, and I have heard said that the evil eye was entered into him.

The men were clumped in groups forward. And to my disgust one of them was standing on the rail, exhorting several around him with a voice of wild fervor; a tall, thin man, hair flying in the wind, cheeks like yellow parchment and a godly eye. Gunner Basil was this, who had a true preaching whine to his Puritan voice.

"No place for you, gunner!" I said when I understood who he was. "Get you aft!"

He rolled his eyes at me and shook his head.

"Nay, nay, sir! It is time that one officer of this ungodly heathen vessel should be able to think for the souls o' these poor men!"

"Your argument may be sound, gunner," I said, "but you had best learn that your place is to obey first and argue later."

With which I clipped him under the ear and took his place at the rail.

"Douse him with a bucket, lads," I said to the men, "and look alive! Where's the bosun? Ah! Damn me if it isn't Bosun Pilcher out of the *Merry Thought*! Bose, remember our voyage in the Guineaman, do you? Glad to find you here, old friend. Watches made up, are they? All taut?"

"Aye, sir, all taut," and Pilcher grinned. A savage brown fellow he was, with golden earrings dangling against his cheeks; short and squat, powerful of build, he was worth dozen men in a pinch.

"What are these preachers we have aboard, bose?" I demanded, looking at he men who stood about. A long-haired lot, with sanctimonious faces and rolling yes.

"Puritans," said Pilcher, and spat over the rail. "Damned if they ain't, sir! It was Mr. Langton shipped the lot. I said 'twas no luck to let a crew be shipped by a Lombard Street merchant, nor is it. Not an oath all mornin', and us a-working like blacks!"

The crew shipped by Langton! I whistled at that. Obviously no one aboard knew anything about Langton's adventures of the morning. Leaving my perch, I took Pilcher's arm and led him forward into the bows, where we might have a quiet word.

"What's this, bose?" I asked. "Say no word of it, but the merchant Langton is being hunted through the city for a pirate. Russel has been on the Account, or I'm a liar! And I'm not so sure about the master —"

"Cap'n Low is the bloodiest of the lot," said Pilcher gloomily. "I'm not s'prised to hear about Langton; not me! Low was piratin' around Madagascar last year. Oh, I'm a wise man, I am! But nobody aboard knows it, d'ye mind, sir! If 'twas not for what we've got stowed aft I'd ha' jumped ship."

"Eh?"

I stared at him.

"What's stowed aft, then?" I asked. He gave me a grin.

"Oh, you don't know, sir? Well, I'll not tell ye. Why Langton went and shipped these here psalm-whining fish I don't know, but that bleedin' Gunner Basil ain't the soapy fool he looks nor acts, Mr. Roberts! You and me are honest men, and the score up for'ard are honest fools; but Gunner Basil ain't one or t'other. D'ye know where I heard tell of him? Far and away it was, last v'yage —"

We leaned against the rail, filled and lighted our pipes, and Bosun Pilcher told me what he knew about our zealous gunner. It was worth the telling.

"D'ye mind, sir, last v'yage 'twas in a Bristol brigantine, to Madeira and the Verde Islands, and back with wine and salt, and a weary time it was, for she leaked like a sieve all the while. We hove out o' Funchal and made for the Isle o' Sal to take our salt aboard, that was in the making; and got safe into the north end of Palmera Roads, and anchored with the palm-trees east-and-by-north, in that spot o' clear sand bottom, five fathom.

"A man came off to us, a white man, marooned there, he had been, by a Frenchman named Maring or some such name, a pirate it was. He told us of a great fight there had been aboard o' the Frenchy six months back, and how there was a famous gunner aboard of her, a gunner by the name o' Basil, full of all pirate learning and a very law-shark for all them that were on the Account. And he said the Frenchy had shot off the lobe of this gunner's ear with a pistol and had set him ashore, all from some dispute over a woman.

"And sink me if this here preacher ain't the identical scoundrel, sir! You look at his ear, and there it be.

"Well, that's not the whole of it neither. This chap told us a long story, which I disremember in the main, but 'twas all about this here Gunner Basil and some wild tale that lay along of he. D'ye mind the pirate Avery? Gunner Basil had sailed with him, and talked in his cups about Avery's treasure that lay buried at one of the Verde

Islands; he knew where the place was, and there be not another living man knew of it, and he was all for going after it. A wild tale enough!"

"Wild, but it might hold truth," I commented. "Avery burned down one of the towns in those islands, and cruised about there. However, what matter to us? This Gunner Basil, you think, is pretending to be a preaching Puritan just now?"

"Aye, to save his neck, belike."

Pilcher shook his earrings.

"Folks do call me a pirate because I wear hoops, and have a roll to my legs on dry land, and have use for an honest oath or two; but zounds! You know me, Master Roberts. I had liefer be me than this cutthroat devil of a Gunner Basil, with his Scripture and Psalms and whine!"

I had to laugh at this, which was true enough. Bosun Pilcher had the looks of a pirate and the life of an honest man; a wife and six children in Jamestown, and a sober, careful record. Gunner Basil, on the other hand, with all the earmarks of a fanatical blue-nosed Puritan, was by repute a devil on the leash.

"Well, bose," I said, knocking out my pipe, "keep a close tongue and wait for what turns up. You'd best look over the capstan and hawse and be ready to up anchor. Tide's almost at the turn, and I see a boat yonder with Mr. Russel coming aboard."

I turned and started aft, having now remembered something mighty important. As I went I encountered Gunner Basil, who touched his forelock to me as I passed and made no comment on my lesson in obedience. Russel's boat was hailing us, and at the break of the poop I found Captain Low waiting for me. I was up the ladder and had him by the arm, fumbling in my pocket.

"Ha, cap'n! I met a friend of yours ashore, and he charged me with word for you —"

Before I could say more, Russel was over the rail and

leaping up to us, his dark face all ablaze with fury and excitement.

"The word's out after Dennis!" he cried, but low-voiced that the men might not hear. "Devil's luck, Ned, devil's luck! Some fool recognized him this morning; put the catch-polls after him! Zounds, if we don't get up the hook and into the Channel they'll twig the whole affair! Up and away, I tell you!"

Ned Low flung a glance at the after companion. His eyes were suddenly stricken.

"Damn me, this is bad news!" he murmured. "And at the last minute!"

"Up and away!" snarled Russel, still panting.

"No, no, I'll not run and leave him!" exclaimed Low warmly; but I intervened.

"Langton isn't nabbed, and won't be," I said, coolly enough, while they stared at me. "I met him ashore, and he had time to give me a message for you, cap'n, before the constables set him running afresh. Said for you to drop downstream with the tide, and he'd come aboard — this side Gravesend, most likely."

"Good!" cried Low.

He snapped erect as if this news had put fresh life into him, and his smile leaped out once more.

"Trust Dennis to come clear! Mr. Russel, be ready to shake out those topsails in five minutes; the tide's nearly at the turn. Mr. Roberts, take charge for'ard and see the anchor's well stowed."

Russel gave me one look that was like a stab; then his white teeth flashed in a laugh.

"So you know Langton, Mr. Roberts!" he said, and nodded. "Good enough. We'll pull together after all."

Oddly, it seemed that his ill will toward me had vanished; this was all seeming, however, because he thought that I was a friend of Langton, and bore this latter some well-founded fear. He was soon enough snarling again.

I went forward while the bosun's whistle shrilled and the men jumped to stations. Everything was shipshape; the men began to stamp about the windlass, capstan bars of dark teak all ashine in the sun, pawls clinking as the ship walked up on her hook, and the canvas aloft beginning to loose. A sweet ship was the *King Sagamore*! Every little detail of her was sweet and natty. Even the fife-rail was of red teak, and the belaying pins of black, heavy as iron.

Now she leaned over to wind and tide and began to slip through the water, while Cap'n Low himself conned her through the river traffic; six bells was struck from the brass bell, and I minded the cabinboy struck them; a slim lad, a guttersnipe of the town, his face pinched and marked with deviltry beyond the ken of most men.

And I noted an odd enough thing. Shoving on the black capstan bars of teak, or hauling on the lines, there was no singing from those men of ours. Instead, not a sound from them until we were bracing the yards a bit, and then one long-nosed rascal began to chant out a psalm, in which they all joined. Damn me, but I can still hear the roar of mirth that went up as a barge passed us and caught the words!

I sent the gunner down to see that all the ports were closed; she carried four guns to a side and six patteroes — a well armed jade! Or, should I say, warrior? The matter of sex is all a jumble when it comes to the *King Sagamore*. Pocahontas would have been a better name for her. This psalm singing was too much for me, however.

"Belay that singing!" I ordered at length. "Bose, pipe 'em the old bowline! Join in you Newgate rascals, or you'll taste trouble!"

So presently Pilcher led them, and the voice of Gunner Basil boomed up the words from below, and the rascals stamped the deck to a right tune:

"Oh, haul upon the bowline, the fore and maintop bowline!
Oh, haul upon the bowline — the bowline, haul!"

And so we had everything snugged down for the present, and I joined Cap'n Low on the quarterdeck, while Russel and the gunner stood at the rail, watching the riverbanks slide past us. Now I went up to Low, who stood at the wheel, and spoke to him softly.

"Ned, I said nothing of it before Russel, but Dennis Langton gave me more than a word for you. Hold out your hand and take the little box."

He dropped a hand to his side, and I put the little black snuffbox into it; and, not taking his eyes from the water ahead, he nodded.

"Good, Roberts!" he said quietly. "So Dennis is playing fair with us, eh? Fine. Ah! Look there, behind those fishing-smacks — is that a boat? Here take my glass."

I took the spyglass from his pocket and leveled it.

"Aye! Two oarsmen and Langton himself in the stern. Now they've seen us —"

"Stand by with a line, Russel!" cried out Low, "Roberts, stand by those braces and be ready. We'll pick him up on the jump."

Pick him up we did, nigh swamping the wherry in the attempt. Langton came up and over the rail, nimble as a cat; but he had not been on the escape for nothing, since his clothes were torn and muddied and his wig clean gone, leaving him bald and shiny.

Nor was this all; for no sooner was he on deck than he staggered and collapsed into the arms of Russel with a choked cry, and I glimpsed a smear of blood across the mate's shoulder. Ned Low saw it too, for he turned to me with a quiet word.

"*Habet*! Lead in the lungs, and that's one of us gone to hell. Crack on all sail, Mr. Roberts! I leave the deck to you.

Get us out o' this cursed water and to sea before they send a man-o'-war to stop us. This is a sad business — the poor girl!"

What he meant by this last, I had no idea, for I was already calling all hands, and Pilcher piped the men to the weather braces and aloft on the instant. Russel and Ned Low carried the figure of Langton to the quarterdeck, and I saw nothing more of them for the time, being mighty busy alow and aloft. Gunner Basil I sent to the helm, needing a good man there if we were to race out of the river. The sails were loosed already, and the men piping down from aloft.

"Haul aboard! Get your tack well down, bose! Tend braces, you lads — set taut! Sheet home — sheet home and hoist away, there! Lead along and man the flying-jib halyards — clear away the downhaul — hoist! All hands main braces —"

So it went, with Pilcher's pipe whistling shrill and the canvas fluttering out. Much to my surprise I perceived that these long-nosed dissenters forward were good enough seamen; and in no long time we were bowling away for dear life, our new canvas straining in the wind and Gunner Basil handling helm in sweet fashion.

Then, with all clear, I turned to the quarterdeck — and stood thunderstruck.

Russel, sitting under the weather rail, held the head of Dennis Langton in his arms, while Ned Low knelt beside and talked to Langton, who was coughing blood. The man had a bullet through the body, and it needed no surgeon to know that his hours were numbered. It was not this, however, that held me transfixed, but the person kneeling over Langton's hand; for this was a woman!

She had come from the after cabins obviously; a straight, slim slip of a thing all yellow golden hair and sober gray gown and long hands. Her face I could not see, but judged that she was young.

A flutter aloft caused me to look at the helmsman. Gunner Basil was staring at the scene, and being down the wind was probably hearing their words. With an angry shout I leaped to the wheel, shoved him away and ordered him to take charge forward. He went, but with a sour snarl in his yellow parchment face.

Indeed, standing in the wheel-box I found that the wind brought me snatches of talk from the group. The girl was sobbing, and Dennis Langton was speaking to her between his terrible coughs. The words reached to me clearly.

Even as I listened, even as I felt the ship with the wheel and held her in the wind, even as I watched shore and opening river-mouth, I was aware of Gunner Basil and that devil-eyed little cabinboy, talking together near the foot of the main; and I wondered vaguely of what they were speaking.

"Keep it, Polly!" came Langton's gasping voice. "All for you — swear — promise me!"

The girl sobbed out something. Without looking at him I was aware that Langton's head lifted, and his eyes leaped to Ned Low.

"Ned, Ned! You'll not take it from her? Aye, you were always on the level — met on the level with us, parted on the square — Ho there, Tyler! Out sword, Tyler; run the knave through! Damn your eyes. Tyler, you missed him! Netting's up and we can't board —"

For a moment he raved, then fell suddenly silent, gasping and sobbing for breath, coughing up the black blood. I stole a glance, and his face was white as beech-ash.

"Call Russel, Ned!" came his voice again. "Where's Russel; John Lopez that was, John Russel that is now?"

"I'm here, Dennis," said the dark mate, bending over so that Langton knew him.

"Swear to me then," gasped the latter. "Swear you'll

give my share to Polly — swear you'll be true to her, not cheat her — swear!"

"Aye," said Russel, whose real name seemed to be Lopez. "I swear it, Dennis, and take the cap'n to witness!"

"Swear it, Ned!" cried out Langton, looking up.

Ned Low, his face set and mournful, inclined his head.

"I'll be true to you and her, Dennis, and will protect her, so help me! I swear it by the oath that you and I know — the oath of the book and compass and word!"

"Where's Roberts, the Virginian?"

Langton's head lifted.

"Call him! Good man, Roberts; true man — stand by him, Ned! I liked that man. Call him — swear him —"

Ned Low strode over to me.

"Give me the helm, and go to him. Quick, man, before he passes!"

I obeyed. Although I was in the dark as to this oath, it appeared honest enough and would soothe the passing of a dying man. As I knelt before Langton, recognition came into his eyes, fighting the fear of death that was filling them.

"Swear, Virginian!" he panted out. "Stand wi' Polly — her share —"

"I swear, Dennis Langton," was my response.

His head dropped back, and a cry came from the girl's throat — then, with a furious and frightful effort, Dennis Langton swept Polly aside, wrenched himself to his feel, swayed there and shook his fist toward London. Laughter and blood came from his lips, and one last wild cry.

"Cheated you, Jack Ketch — cheated you first and last, Tyburn Tree! Sink me to hell if I haven't the laugh o' you after all! Zounds!"

He rattled on the word, and died, and pitched forward with a laugh terrible on his lips. Thus passed the first of our company aboard the *King Sagamore*; and as I watched Russel take the weeping girl to the companionway I wondered to what oath I had sworn myself, in the hand of a dying pirate.

CHAPTER III

While we pitched and rolled down-Channel that night I was below with Ned Low, seeing that Dennis Langton was properly sewed up for burial. Gunner Basil brought a shot for his feet and then, touching his forelock, respectfully enough addressed us; in the light of the swinging lantern his parchmenty face looked more yellow and wolfish than ever.

"Beg pardon, masters, but who's a-goin' to say the prayer over him?" he asked.

"I am."

Ned Low glanced up.

"Why?"

"It ain't fittin', sir," protested the gunner with an air of earnest, stubborn conviction.

His pale, deadly eyes were fastened upon Low.

"He died in sin, most like, but it ain't fittin' for you to say no prayer, sir. It's the spirit movin' me to protest."

Ned Low straightened up.

"Now, sink me! I'm master o' this ship —"

"We that has a higher hope don't hold wi' no blasphemy; beg pardon, master, what be you but an ungodly, unregenerate sinner? Blasphemy it is, no less. More'n one of us aboard ha' heard tell o' 'Bloody Ned,' cap'n. Tha' ain't here nor there; but when it comes to sayin' prayers, I speaks up! It's the spirit movin' in me —"

Bloody Ned! Well, there it was, like a slap in the face. I had heard of Bloody Ned, too, but had not connected the name with my good friend Captain Ned Low.

For a moment I thought Ned would strike the man down. Eyes clenched with eyes, and in the obscurity behind Gunner Basil I perceived more than one dark figure lurking. Then in time I recalled the tale that Bosun Pilcher had told me, and pushed forward with a nudge in Low's ribs.

"What's all this?" I demanded. "This is fine talk from you, Basil, who were on the Account with Avery and served as his gunner! And what about that French pirate you sailed with — the one who pistoled you and marooned you after the big fight, eh?"

There was dead silence, broken only by the groan of stanchions and the creak of blocks. My knowledge of his past took Gunner Basil all aback; he gaped at me from a livid and stricken face. Ned Low uttered a soft oath of astonishment. A murmur began to rise from the listening men. I struck again while the iron was hot.

"A prayer would come with ill grace from you, gunner — as lief from Bloody Ned as from Avery's gunner, if I'm the victim! Who was it nicked the lobe off that ear of yours with a pistol ball, eh?"

Gunner Basil staggered again at that thrust. I felt a swift stab of fear as I met those pale eyes of his; then he began to shake his long head and whine.

"When a man repenteth him of the evil and turns to godliness, the scornful make mock of him! Aye, sir, you ha' the right of it; a sinful man I ha' been, and taken part wi' men o' blood. And now that regeneration ha' come upon me, by the works o' the blessed Tom Deveney o' Houndsditch —"

"Regeneration your eye, ye damned lousy swab of a liar!" broke in a roar, and Bosun Pilcher lurched forward. "Who was it a-throwin' oaths so free and fine but a half hour ago? You, ye scabby sojer, thinkin' no one was by to hear! Now out knife if ye dare, and I'll show ye summat —"

It looked like blows and hot breath, for Pilcher had hand on knife and Gunner Basil was clutching under his arm; but Ned Low stepped forward and stood between the two men and reasserted his command.

"Damn me, d'ye think we're on the Account, to settle quarrels wi' the steel!" he cried out. "Out o' this, bose! You, gunner, give me no more of your sanctimonious lip, d'ye hear? You'll taste a dozen of the cat next time. Get this boy made ready, and five bells in morning watch call all hands for burial. Mr. Roberts, it's hard on eight bells — you'd better step up and stand by to take the deck from Mr. Russel."

"From Portugee Lopez, ye mean," shot a voice out of the shadows. "Lopez, the bloody pirate what scuppered three Deal craft last year!"

"Who was that?" snapped Ned Low, hand dropping to belt. "Out of the dark, you rat! Who was it?"

None answered him, however, and the darkness proved empty to the swing of a lantern. So I went on deck again, wondering not a little. That voice had held an odd twang, not unlike the tones of the impish cabinboy, but that was impossible. The child stood in deadly fear of us all and was seasick to boot.

With a fair wind, ballast trimmed anew and one of our brawny dissenters at the helm, we bore down-Channel into the darkness; while I, after lighting my pipe in the lee of the pilothouse, reflected a while upon my situation. It might have been worse, what I knew of it, and it might assuredly have been bettered. Certain outstanding things looked dark.

One certainty was that in London town I had run foul of three fine rogues, and like a blockhead had been hooked. Langton's end spoke for itself. Russel, or Portuguese Lopez, obviously had something of a reputation as a pirate. Of Bloody Ned I had heard, and was grieved to find it was my own Ned Low, the man whom I so liked. As to the girl Polly, I had not seen or heard of her again, but she seemed to be some relation to Langton.

Why had these three men outfitted and chartered — as they must have done — the *King Sagamore*? To get gold from the Cape Verde Islands, Ned Low had said.

All very fine; but how? There was the puzzler. They had not meant to run away with her and go on the Account.

Langdon in his capacity as a city merchant had probably given bonds for her, and he had most certainly picked the crew himself. These men were godly rogues, and I did not like them in the least — but they were honest men. Langton would never have picked such a crew to ship as pirates.

Then again there was the question of Gunner Basil. Captain Low had been utterly astounded at learning the gunner's record; he had known nothing of it. Ergo, Dennis Langton had known nothing of it and had shipped the gunner at face value.

But why the hell had Gunner Basil shipped aboard us? I took no stock in his "regeneration" — one look in the man's eyes clapped a stopper on all that. He could fool the men up forward, but he could not fool me, much less Bosun Pilcher.

And what was that oath I had taken? It disquieted me.

I had reached this point, and two bells had just been struck, when the tall figure of Ned Low approached. He glanced at the compass, lighted his pipe, then took my arm and led me to the lee rail, where we could speak without being overheard.

"Roberts, I've been talking with John Russel, and I'm worried," he said frankly and bluntly. "This morning, standing on the quay, you as good as told Russel you'd been on the Account yourself. Tonight you flashed some information on Gunner Basil that staggered him — and me with him. How came you to know it, lad? If you've lied to me, then let's have it out sharp and quick, and reach an understanding."

This was a stiff jolt, and I let him know it.

"About Russel, that was said in jest, to taunt him. As to the rest, Ned — well, I learned tonight that you are Bloody Ned. It grieved me, but I didn't come running and whining to ask if the news was true. Zounds! If I'm such a fool that I can't read a man's eye for true or false, it's a queer thing. And I'll stick by my guns, swing me if I don't!"

Low caught my hand and gripped it hard.

"Spoken like a man, George Roberts!" he said warmly. "Aye, and with a bitter back to the words that I deserve! Your pardon, lad. We'll have a meeting in the cabin tomorrow morning after breakfast, all four of us, and you'll know then why I'm anxious."

"Who's the fourth, then?" I asked.

"Polly Langton, niece and heir of poor Dennis. That was a stiff loss to us, George! Dennis had a head worth any two going,"

"He'd not much when he shipped our gunner," I said acidly.

Ned Low whistled.

"Perchance. But the scoundrel may ha' told truth after all, lad; there's a chance of that, d'ye mind! Men have reformed ere this, and will again. Why, look at me, myself!"

He was silent for a moment, then took me across the deck again and under the weather rail, where we sat down in comfort. I think he had been much moved by my challenging answer to his doubts; at least he spoke with a refinement and feeling in his voice that I had not previously heard.

"Roberts, y'have never seen or heard, I suppose, of a man calling himself Trunnel Toby, having a long face like a horse, and sad eyes, and a gold ring in his nostrils, and the likeness of a bleeding heart tattooed upon his breast, just above his own heart?"

"Not I," was my answer.

"I have sought that man going on five years," said Ned Low. "Once I knew that his ship lay in Carlisle Bay, and I sighted her plain; but there was a gale blowing, and we were short of men, and before we could hand the small sails and luff for the bay we were driven past, and the gale held us, and when I came back again he was gone. Oh, but I ha' tried with heart and soul to find that man, all up and down the dark bowl of the sea!

"And once I was within an hour of him. At Madagascar that was; aye, missed him by a scant sixty minutes, though I caught three of his men left behind, and hanged them! He had heard of Bloody Ned, and he ran for it. And off the Zanzibar coast I met a ship that had spoke him two days before, and north we ran and passed him in a hurricane, and he came over to the Brazils for fear o' me. Now and again, and every way, I found men who had sailed with him, men who had partnered or traded with him, and I hanged them all as I came on them.

"But I never found Trunnel Toby, and ha' lost hope of finding the man now, so I am off to recoup my wasted fortune again, and search some more. The last o' my guineas are in this ship, Roberts; and a big sum from poor Langton, and a share from John Russel. And I am afraid to ask Gunner Basil if he knew the man, for if he did I would hang him, and we have need of a gunner aboard. Besides the man may have reformed, as he says; I'd put it past no man to turn righteous.

"For look you, George! There is a reason behind all of us. Aye, there's a reason back of each man who dares this wine-dark sea and listens to the rigging as it sings the slumbering song o' night up above! Lord knows I've earned the name of Bloody Ned, earned it with hangings of men alow and aloft — but all of them men who had known Trunnel Toby, d'ye mind that!

"And I've naught to repent of at all, either. I've

touched no man's life but for this cause; I've touched no man's money but mine own, honestly made.

"And poor Langton, to whom that gunner laid his tongue, had become an honest man. D'ye know why, George? Because of the girl down below, his niece Polly; and she's a rare lass, I tell you! Bred of the Devon blood, she is, and can hand sail with any man or read the card or steer by the wind. So when I came and said that I was for the gold and had given up the search for Trunnel Toby until we had the guineas again, Langton knew it was an honest word and came in with me; and John Russel made up the sum we lacked, and we bought this ship, George."

"Bought her!" I said in some wonder, for that would have taken round money.

"Aye, just so. A company venture for the gold. We'll have it again soon enough, and then I'll buy out the other shares and keep the *King Sagamore* and go again after Trunnel Toby. Sure y'have never heard of the man?"

"Never," I said. "But there's Bosun Pilcher come to look at the helm; call him, for many a thing he has heard and seen, and an honest man to boot."

Ned Low lifted his voice, and the dark shadow of bose detached itself from the pilot-box and came over to us on the sloping deck. So there Ned Low asked his question again, and described the man he sought. Bose turned the quid in his mouth and chewed upon it and spat over the stern rail, and then made careful answer.

"Why, sir, there be many a man wi' face like a horse, and one or two aboard here, but not that man. Seems like I've heard tell of he, too; let's see now — was it aboard the *Merry Thought*? No, 'twas not; yet 'twas not so long ago —

"Ha! Damn me eyes, sir, if 'twas not two v'yages back, on the *Pricket* brigantine, wi' Cap'n Baxter out o' Bristol town! I mind it well enough now. We were lying at Lisbon, and a supra-cargo there was tellin' me of such a man, bleedin' heart and all! Mate on a London trading-brig, he was, and had got into trouble wi' the Portugee folk, and had skipped between two days. That's where I heard the name, and more'n that I can't bring to mind."

"Then let it pass," said Ned Low, sinking back against the rail.

"Aye, sir," said bose. "Four bells it is, sir."

"Make it so, bose," I told him, and he went off into the darkness.

The brazen tinkle of the bell had died away before Ned Low spoke again.

"And what think you, George," he said, "of sailing mate with Bloody Ned?"

I laughed a little at that.

"What else but your own words, Ned? We're not on the Account, but for honest gold, you say; and enough said. There's a reason behind every man sails up the sea, you say; and enough said. For the rest, I like you, I have two fists, and if I go to the devil it's my own fault and no other man's leading."

"Well said, George. What reason is behind you?"

"Ruined fortunes, a girl who jilted me, and lack of ties to keep me ashore. Those in the first place. In the latter place, love of good ships, work to do and strength to do it with, and knowledge of my profession. For I hold the sea to be a profession, Ned, in despite of all men! I sailed a small sloop with two boys from the Azores to Barbados once to prove the fact. What was more, I built the sloop before sailing her."

"You're a philosopher, George, and damn me if I don't wish I might be one too!" he responded, and sighed. "Work to do, and strength and knowledge to do it with! What more could any man ask of fortune? But my work's undone as yet, and when done it's only a man hanged after all, and small joy of it to me!"

With this he rose, and was gone down below.

I wondered much about his words and his curious

tale of Trunnel Toby, and what reason must lie behind his strange pursuit of that creature up and down the waters of the earth. Reason in plenty there must be, but I could not evoke it from his words. It began to appear, however, that he was not the black pirate he was painted, and this was something to cheer me.

So the night wore through, and the wind held fair, sweeping us steadily to the southward on our course, and with the dawn or a little while after we gathered all hands in the waist. Now all the world was shut away from us. We aboard the *King Sagamore*, bounded by those walls of English oak and India teak, were in a little world apart, devils and angels and men together. There was the dead man, shrouded decently; and by him Ned Low, book in hand, and dark, quick-eyed Russel, dirk and pistol in belt, and Gunner Basil, pale, terrible eyes flaming and stabbing about. Little love those pale eyes bore me, either!

There, too, Bosun Pilcher, gold earrings bobbing beside savage brown cheeks, and back of him the men, making a full score of us, all told. Some I had come to know by this time. Dickon the cabinboy, gray with the sickness and mouthing vile oaths; Simon Blake and Ezra Blake his brother, gaunt, hard-jawed fellows who could prate psalms by the hour; and Philip the cook, a black man who was very joyful about his work and always grinning. Humphrey Stave was chips and sail-maker, a bent gnarled figure with deep eyes behind spectacles, and a bit deaf; Stave was the only other man forward who was not a man of religion and godliness, so that he companioned much with Pilcher.

The others were all hard men, devout enough and good seamen, but given to exhorting each other with prayer and advice. Dennis Langton had picked them for this very reason, having no mind to ship pirates on this voyage.

None the less, he had made a mistake. One of the

men, Thomas Winter, was long in the face, a real horse's face indeed, seeming but little short of a halfwit, nor ever raised his eyes to meet those of another man.

Well, we buried poor Dennis Langton there, sliding him off into the rolling seas; and after reading the proper service Ned Low softly asked the gunner to speak a prayer. Gunner Basil did so, praying a good ten minutes in a long, whining singsong, the other knaves all joining in with their nasal "Amen" when the spirit moved.

Then breakfast, and then to the cabin for the promised meeting, while Gunner Basil held the deck. And in this meeting I had sight of Polly Langton and likewise got a bid from fortune.

CHAPTER III

We gathered in the stern cabin, and the new sunlight streamed down through the small skylight above and illumined the cabin with a glory of radiance as the ship rolled. Between stern window and skylight we had plenty of light.

The cabin was not ornate. It was our mess cabin aft, and was meant for use, not for ornament. Along the stern wall under the window ran a long file of muskets, locked in their rack by an iron bar and padlock. A locker for charts, another for instruments; a huge cupboard that held dishes and wine and other things; table and chairs and iron lantern slung in gimbals — this was all. Under the table was a trap leading to the lazaret below.

With the traces of grief gone from her cheeks Polly Langton sat down, and we after her. For lack of mourning she wore her gray gown; a kerchief about her throat fastened by a gold brooch; and what a head was this rising above! All a glory of yellow gold hair, and a red-cheeked, west-country face that was filled with sweetness and ability, browned by the sun and air, with skin delicately textured as any court lady's!

Yet the splendor of her face lay in the eyes; gray with golden flecks were they, level and meeting a man's gaze fair and unafraid; deliberate eyes, not to be hurried or overborne. Through these windows one perceived the fine woman's soul within, shrinking a little, yet meeting the issues of fate with a certain cool poise that was almost disdain. Could this girl ever be waked into hot passionate anger or emotion, I thought, she would stop at nothing!

Painted and powdered, patched and gowned, Polly

Langton might have been no beauty; but in her simplicity she was beautiful enough. I did not miss the grip that was in Russel's eyes as he watched her; nor did she; for she gave him a slow look that made him change countenance.

Ned Low, when we were seated, put on the table before him that little black snuffbox which I had brought him from Langton. Then Russel spoke up, civilly but with a thrust to his words.

"One minute, cap'n! This is secret company business. Why does George Roberts sit with us?"

"At my bidding," and Ned Low smiled a little, taking no offense. "He is my friend, and I trust him to the full. Also I propose that he is to have a full third of my share of the gold when recovered —"

"I want no gifts, Ned," I intervened.

"No gift at all, George Roberts," he returned, a somber look in his eyes. "We don't know what lies ahead of us, but I think you are going to be a great man in this enterprise, and here you, a captain like myself, are serving as mate. Zounds, man! Was it not agreed between us that first night we met?"

"As to that I can't say," was my response, and Ned uttered a laugh.

"It's a company matter," spoke up Russel, an ugly note in his voice. "Put it to the vote, I say!"

"It's no company matter what I do with my own," snapped Low angrily, a dark color rising in his cheeks. "But the deciding voice lies with Miss Polly, and I put the vote. What say you, madam?"

All this while the girl had been looking at me with appraising eyes. Now she leaned back in her chair and spoke as if she had no interest in the affair.

"I agree," she said quietly, "though it is your own business, as you say."

So Russel sat back and bit his lip.

"Now," began Ned Low, "let us inform Captain Roberts of our quest. You've heard of the pirate Franklin, George? Some time since, I was in company with him when he took a huge amount of moidores out of a Portugee Indiaman from Goa."

He broke off, for the girl was holding his eye. He flushed a trifle once more.

"Then it is true," she asked coolly, "that you and Mr. Russel were on the Account, as they call it?"

"That is true," said Ned. "It is also true that I would touch no penny of the loot, my lady. Then I had no use for it. Now I have use. Captain Franklin buried a great share of the gold, which he swore belonged to me, on one of the Verde Islands. He and I alone knew the place. It is this gold that we go to recover.

"According to the agreement, a third share goes to me, another to John Russel, another to Mistress Langton here. Out of my share, a third goes to Captain Roberts. This is understood and agreed?"

A nod came from the other two. But now Polly Langton spoke up — cool and well-considered words; and her speech must have come as a tremendous shock to each one of us.

"Since Captain Roberts is a friend of yours, Captain Low, and is to share in your proceeds, he is evidently tarred with the same brush as you and Mr. Russel! By your own word you are pirates. How my poor uncle came to his death I know not, but I think it was through entering into this scheme of yours.

"Shame on you! He was an honest city merchant, and you bloody men tangled him in your ruthless wiles! Had it not been for you we would still be living in Lombard Street, and happy there."

She paused, coldly deliberate. Ned Low was staring at her like a man thunderstruck. John Russel was all agape, but harsh amusement was rising in his eyes. Before it could break out she was calmly continuing her speech.

"I promised my uncle to take this gold if we got it. What I do with my share is another matter, I may be penniless, but beyond taking out what my poor uncle put into this venture, I'll not turn this bloody coin to my own use.

"Very well, then. I want it understood plainly that I'm a full third partner in this enterprise, and intend to remain so. I'm not to be put in a corner and disregarded because I am a woman. My uncle picked a good crew for this voyage; if you gentlemen think you can run away with this ship or go pirating, you'll discover otherwise. We are here for a certain purpose, and none other."

Now her voice softened — perhaps from what she read in the eyes of Ned Low.

"Indeed I do not mean to speak like a shrew, but there's the fact. You're pirates. I am a woman, but I have some ability at sea. The crew are honest men. I think you mean me well, and will respect the oath which you gave my poor uncle; but I want to have things understood. Already the men are whispering that you intend running away with the ship. Be careful! That's all. I am through, Captain Low."

There was a space of silence, while we stared at her. It was easy to perceive that Dennis Langton had kept her ignorant of his past. She thought him a good, honest merchant, not knowing that he had buccaneered with the worst of them, had partnered with the infamous Spriggs. She was acting upon genuine belief, deeming the rest of us mighty insecure men.

Russel uttered a laugh and began to speak, a sneer in his heavy eyes. Ned Low turned to him, face set and cold, and uttered three words —

"Be silent, John!"

Russel checked himself, shrugged and leaned back grinning. Thus the matter passed; Ned was trying to keep from the poor girl the knowledge of what her uncle had been, was trying to leave her memory of him unsoiled. Yet he was a fool for his pains. She was bound to learn the truth eventually.

"Since I haven't known you or your friends three days, Miss Polly," I said easily, "you can't charge me with their crimes. My record is clear for all men to read, and if you'll go out to Virginia you'll find that it's not a bad record either. And as to Captain Low, I believe you'll find that he's —"

"Stow it, George!" snapped Low.

I obeyed, for he was angry.

He looked across the table at the girl, and she at him, though her gaze had softened a bit. Very handsome he was, and too proud to take notice of her words. He opened the black snuffbox that lay before him and took out the hard, folded bit of vellum, all the while keeping his eyes on the girl. And then he spoke to her briefly.

"Dear lady, you have naught to fear from us, upon my honor! Now let us to business. I propose to lay this little chart before you — Franklin himself made it — and then destroy the thing. We shall keep the position of the moidores in our own minds. If by any chance of the sea we do not reach the Verde Islands, then whichever one of us can first come to the spot is at liberty to take the gold."

There was a little silence while he opened up the vellum. It was not easy, for the whitish skin was hard and dry and promised to crack at the folds. As he opened it slowly, I saw that on one side of it was writing, and that over the ink there had been wax laid on and polished, keeping the ink waterproof.

Then abruptly the voice of the girl leaped at us. Soft it was, but uttered in broad Devon that betrayed her apprehension and fear.

"Quick! Catch mun — look to door!"

She said afterward that the door-catch had moved slightly. Russel saw it, for he was out of his chair, silent and with a stealthy agility that amazed me, and in two steps was at the door. He opened it. There came a terrific crash as a tray dropped to the floor, and we saw Dickon the cabinboy outside.

Russel had him by the shoulder and heaved him inside and swore at the ale that spattered his feet.

"What means this, lad?" demanded Ned Low angrily. "Who bade you listen at doors?"

The little imp was no whit in awe or frightened, he faced us in stiller defiance. He could not have seen fifteen years, yet the debased evil of his features would have done credit to any pirate, and he glowered at us with all the hatred of a man for men.

"It bain't so," he said stoutly. "I weren't a-listening, Master Low! Cook Philip sent me wi' breakfast for mistress — and now look at un! Pewter bent, ale gone —"

Russel gave him a hearty cuffing and threw him out into the passage. As the boy picked himself up I saw the look he flung at Russel — a deadly, vicious look such as comes from the eyes of a disturbed and angry snake. Then Russel slammed the door shut and came back to his chair.

"I was mistaken," spoke up Polly contritely. "I thought perhaps someone was listening — I'm sorry if little Dickon suffered for my error."

"He's not hurt," said Russel. "Now, Ned, out with it! Which one of the islands is it?"

"St. Vincent," answered Captain Low, holding the vellum spread out under his fingers. "You know it?"

"I've not landed there," said Russel.

"Franklin has it marked 16°49' north latitude, by 7°6' west longitude from the Cape de Verde," went on Ned Low, "but I think he's off a point or two. George, get out the charts, will you? We'll show Miss Polly just where we're going."

I got out the proper chart, by which time the others were ready to relinquish the bit of vellum to me, though Russel watched me keenly while I handled it. Upon it was rudely scratched the outline of St. Vincent, one of several uninhabited and rocky islands to the northwest of the Cape Verde group. On the northeast tip of the island was marked a cross, with the bearings below. I uttered an exclamation.

"Upon my word, gentlemen! I remember this place; I was there for turtle while we were making salt at the Isle de Sal! Aye, the very spot — and we had best lay up the ship in the cove at the north side of the island, which is the closest."

"It is ill spoke of on the chart," said Russel, looking up.

"Aye, for the trades blow square into it," I assented. "But a ship may be towed out by boats during the morning calm. I've seen the St. Nicholas men do it often. And the bay is so smooth that you may lay a ship ashore without the least damage."

"Memorize those bearings, George," said Ned Low. "We must destroy the thing."

That was an easy matter, the more so that I knew the exact spot. The northeast side of the island, unlike the rest, is low and sandy. A cable-length off the shore at low tide is a round, smooth rock that rises like a broken column out of the water to the height of ten feet; Franklin had marked it "Tower Rock," and there could be no mistake. Bearing from this due west a quarter mile were a group of dragon-trees.

Now I recalled these trees quite clearly, since they were the only group of this species which had escaped destruction, and I was interested in their singular nature and had even visited them, getting some of the gum. Half a cable-length to the west-and-by-north of these trees was a large boulder jutting out of the sand, and the gold was buried on the north side of that boulder.

So said the vellum, and you may judge of my interest in the matter, and of how the others were interested to hear me tell of the place as I knew it, though I did not recall that boulder. Franklin had been a few points amiss on his bearings of the island, but that was nothing. He certainly was not astray on his local features.

"Do you think," Polly Langton asked me, a sparkle in her eyes, "that anyone might have come there and found the treasure?"

"Not unless he were looking for it," I told her. "No one comes to that island except for turtle, or to shoot wild goats, or to fish. The black island men from St. Nicholas come there often, but they make no stay. There is fresh water in a large bay on the northwest side the island — Porto Grande it is called."

"Aye, it is marked."

Ned Low rolled up the big chart.

"Russel," he went on, "have you finished with the bearings? And you, George? And you, Miss Polly?"

We had it all in our heads, well enough. So Captain Low struck a light, and presently the white vellum curled and crumpled and became a black ash on the table. Then Low looked up at us, and laughed in his gay manner.

"And now, comrades, a sneaker to our good luck and fortune!"

He brought wine and flagons from the cupboard, and we pledged Franklin's gold, the girl with a flash to her eye and color to her cheek. Then, since Polly Langton had not yet broken her fast, I went to hasten Dickon with his second tray, and so took charge of the deck. And this ended our conference.

We had now no further talk among ourselves of the gold, for it was a dangerous matter, and would keep well enough until we arrived at the spot. With the next morning indeed foul weather came upon us; not contrary, but heavy gales that swept us on our course yet kept all hands on the jump. Day after day they continued unabated, and the *King Sagamore*, for all her battering and straining, leaked no more water than could be got rid of in an hour's pumping of mornings.

During those days we were too busy to have much time for mischief, which in the light of after events I think was most fortunate. There was indeed some preaching and ranting up forward, but since it gave the men an outlet we made no objection, even when Gunner Basil made long-winded discourses of a Sabbath.

What with the ship's roll, few of us were not seasick at times, and I saw little of

Polly Langton these days. What little I did see, however, woke in me admiration for her bearing and character and spirit. I think she had ceased to class me with pirates, for she was smiling and merry when we met, and sometimes took the wheel during my watch on deck, fighting it with the skill of any man among us.

Dickon the cabinboy was quite sick during this period, which was another fortunate thing in my opinion. We replaced him for the time with Thomas Winter, the long-faced halfwit of whom I have spoken. A curious man was that, who seldom spoke, never met the level look of an eye, and mingled not at all with the other men. He had been long at sea; his hands and forearms were much tattooed; yet none could get him to speak of his goings and comings. He had a vacancy in his aspect that surely belied his wits.

This fellow Winter, also, seemed to be taken with strange spells. One day at noon we had a fleeting glimpse of the sun, and after shooting him with Low I hastily left the deck and jumped below to make calculations and verify our reckoning. As I came into the cabin I found Gunner Basil there, and the man Thomas Winter was speaking to him. I had chance to hear only a few words, but those were spoken in a new voice to me — a sane and sound and bellowing voice.

"Why, damn your eyes!" Winter was roaring at the

gunner. "Who are you to tell me what to do, you whelp of Satan? You stow your jaw, blast you! I'm the one —"

He broke off at sight of me, and cringed. I was the more astonished, for Gunner Basil seemed to be taking his oaths with shamefaced manner.

"What's this?" I broke in upon them. "Winter, was that you I heard? What d'ye mean?"

"Pardon, sir," he mumbled. "They roarin' winds do fetch gusty words out o' me at times, sir, and all o' seven devils a-perched up aloft!"

He shambled away out of the cabin. Gunner Basil looked at me, wagged his head sorrowfully and tapped his skull. He let out his nasal whine.

"Bear with him, sir; bear with him! The poor afflicted fellow deserves the patience of all men. If he is a bit daft, he is also a good seaman — can hold her by the wind wi' never a flutter o' canvas from hour to hour!"

With an impatient word I settled down to my figures. Afterward I remembered again the complete change of voice and language which had been effected in the daft man, and how he had cringed at sight of me. This wakened my pity, and I thought no more of the incident.

CHAPTER 11

Fair weather came back to us as suddenly as it had departed, and found us well advanced on our course, though much strained and battered about. Within two days all our sick were recovered, and we fell to work overhauling the rigging as we sailed, for the new cordage had stretched abominably and must be re-pitched into the bargain.

Hardly had we come into clear skies, however, than trouble let loose aft, as if it had been waiting for fine weather before breaking.

We were heeling smartly along under a spanking breeze out of the northeast-and-by-east, everything drawing well, and four bells of the afternoon had just struck. Old Humphrey Stave was seated by the for'ard water-butt, working with palm and needle at a spare topsail when the bosun appeared and talked for a little with his crony. Then Pilcher came aft, touched his forelock, begged some tobacco from me and fell into talk. He had something at the back of his mind, but was slow in leaching it.

"Cook be heatin' of some pitch in the galley," he observed, "when you're ready to get that for'ard rigging painted, sir."

Simon Blake was at the wheel.

"When it's ready," I said, "send a man aft to relieve Simon here, and let him and Ezra Blake take up the buckets. They're good careful men, and I don't want the deck spattered."

"Aye, sir."

Pilcher shook his earrings, then gave me a queer look.

"There be some wild talk for'ard, sir," he went on.

"What about, bose?"

"That you've been on the Account, sir, and I give the lie to it. But that bain't all. I don't like them there godly men, nor they me; but I've heard whispers. They do say as you and Mr. Russel and Mr. Low ain't doin' right by the lass, and that she's mortal afraid o' you gentlemen. Then there's summat about Mr. Russel bein' one Portugee Lopez, and it bain't no secret that Mr. Low is Bloody Ned —"

"Who's doing this talk?" I demanded, frowning.

We were beyond earshot of the helmsman.

"That I don't know, sir; just driftin' it is. These godly scum for'ard seem to think they'll be made turn pirate."

"We'll work it out of 'em," I said cheerfully. "Run along and attend to that pitch now."

He swung forward. Barely had he gone when from below came Polly Langton and Captain Low. They flung me a bare nod, then resumed some talk they had started below decks, and I saw that the girl was flushed and earnest, while poor Ned Low was cold and set and hard in the face. They paused by the windward rail, so that their words came to me and to Simon Blake, at the wheel.

"And have you no shame for it?" demanded the girl hotly.

"Shame?"

Ned uttered a curt, bitter laugh.

"By the Lord Harry, no! If I'd hanged twice a hundred men, and knew that twice that number would yet die to my hand, I'd go on to the end and be proud of it!"

"I am sorry to hear such words on your lips," and she spoke gravely, her anger held down. "I had thought you a gentleman, and I find you glorying in your bloody deeds, in your piracies and murders! Go on to the end, you say. Do you dare admit that your share of this enterprise is to be used in the same fashion — that if the venture succeeds, if you buy out this ship from our company, you go on the Account once more?"

I cursed under my breath, for Simon Blake was drinking all this in, as his dour face testified; yet I dared not intervene.

"Aye," said Ned Low. "I'll not lie to you, Miss Polly."

"Oh, shame on you!" she cried out. "To think that you and your precious friends so inveigled my poor uncle! You and they, to take this money and use if for more piracy and murder — how do I know you and they will respect that oath to my uncle?"

"Why, take us on trust!"

Ned broke into a laugh, half vexed, half of whimsical exasperation.

"As for my friends, I care not and know not what they'll do with their share. My share puts Bloody Ned on his feet again, madam, and that's my own affair."

She gave him a long look, eyes angry, bosom heaving.

"Then I am minded to draw out of this venture, sir."

"You can't."

Low turned on her, pressed beyond endurance.

"This is a company matter, my girl — don't try to make trouble! There's more behind it all than you know. There's more hangs on it than you know. We'll see you safe in London again with your share; and beyond that — have a care! This gold o' Franklin's belongs to all of us, mind, not you alone."

Now, whether she had meant her threat I know not, but Simon Blake caught his breath sharply, and his face was set in grim lines. But the girl laughed out right merrily under the angry gaze of Ned Low — perhaps she had only meant to tease him, after all. Then she turned and went below without more speech, while Ned fell to pacing the quarterdeck.

It was a moment after this that Thomas Winter, who was in my watch, came shambling aft to relieve Simon

Blake from his trick. A few words passed between them. I stepped up, and Winter repeated the order to go for'ard and tar the lines. Blake nodded assent and obeyed.

I followed forward, as Simon and Ezra Blake secured their buckets and brushes, and came to a pause beside the water-butt, where Humphrey Stave sat and sewed.

"Do those buntlines and the forelift first," I told them, "then work in along the yards from each side, and do the shrouds as you come down. Simon, overhaul that loose foot-rope at the strap, on the fore-yard; tighten it up and watch your seizing."

"Aye, sir," responded Simon, passing the lanyard of his bucket about his neck.

The two men mounted, and a moment later I turned to find Ned Low at my elbow. He gave me a whimsical glance, and chuckled softly.

"Caught the bastard, and no mistake, eh? You heard?"

I nodded.

"Aye, Ned. So did Blake, at the helm. The men for'ard are talking already about things."

"Oh, trice up a couple and give 'em a dozen apiece," he said carelessly, "and there'll be no more gossip. Somebody's been talking to the lass, though, and I don't like it. John Russel has his eye on her. You watch sharp, lad."

"Well, Humphrey Stave, how goes it with the palm? Man, that's as neat a patch as ever I saw laid!"

Old Humphrey squinted up over his spectacles.

"Aye, master, and thankee! You'm be good judge of un, sir."

For a moment Low stood glancing around the deck. What he saw in that swift, eaglelike glance of his, I never knew. But suddenly his hand fell on my arm, and his voice sounded in my ear. Ah, the urgency, the repressed fury, of that voice!

"Quick, for the love of Heaven! Loaded pistols in the

chart locker. Get Russel and the gunner. Don't run aft, now — easy does it —"

My blood jumped. I turned and walked aft, seeking as I did so what had caused his abrupt alarm and caution. Except that most of the port watch were on deck sunning themselves I could see nothing out of the ordinary. The men seemed to eye me hard as I passed aft, but that might have been imagination. The quarterdeck was empty, save for the long figure of Thomas Winter at the helm.

Once at the companionway I was down the ladder with a leap, and darted aft to the cabin. Russel was doubled up in my cabin; I paused to fling open the door.

"John! Up and arm — quick, man!"

He had his own arms, and usually wore them, so I darted on into the main cabin and in the chart locker came upon two pistols, loaded and pinned. I ran back, found Russel sitting on the edge of his bunk and blinking at me, and swore at him.

"On deck! Swift about it!"

I ran on down the passage and came to the companion ladder. As I started up it, something flew out of the darkness below — a knife, that whanged into the wood beyond my ear with a vicious song. Who flung it I could not see and dared not pause to ask, for I was in fear of what might be happening forward.

Up the ladder and to the deck again, and just in time to see it happen!

They thought me gone below, of course, thought Ned Low alone there among them, the dogs! As my head came up, I saw the thing fall — saw the bucket, heavy with pitch, leave the hand of Simon Blake and go hurtling down from the topsail yard. Low did not see it, but he saw Bosun Pilcher gape upward and heard Pilcher cry out and leap aside blindly.

There was a terrible dull sound, and old Humphrey Stave threw out his arms and bent forward across his sail with his skull stove in. Another and more frightful cry burst from Pilcher; I saw the bosun lean back, saw his arm curl and straighten, saw his knife go flaming up through the air.

"Take it, ye damned murderer of old men!" he yelled out, and Simon Blake took it fair in the throat, and pitched off the yard clear of the ship's side.

Now there was a heave of men over Pilcher; and I, running forward, saw Ezra Blake lean over from the futtock shrouds and drop his own heavy bucket toward Ned Low. The latter, warned by my shout, leaped aside once more and the bucket missed. I flung up one pistol and shot the treacherous hound, and he fell straight at the foot of the foremast, where men were rearing cutlasses from the rack.

Then Ned Low was into them with both hands, and as one man swung at him with a blade I fired again and that man fell. All this, and the body of Ezra dropping among them, and the sight of me running forward, with John Russel behind me and the gunner also on deck, gave them pause.

Pilcher broke loose and stood beside the captain, and I joined them. Then came Russel leaping like a hound across the deck with a pistol in one hand and knife in the other, and a wild grin upon his dark face. Behind him came Gunner Basil, long hair flying, pale eyes darting about.

"Up with those cutlasses again, ye dogs!" shouted Low, and they obeyed sullenly. "So it's mutiny, is it — murder and mutiny, ye swine of righteousness! You there about the arms rack, stand fast!"

Four of the men there were, still half determined to fly at us, and Low held out his hand toward them.

"Gunner Basil! Trice up those four devils. Bose, pipe all hands and give those rascals two dozen."

One of the other men stepped forward defiantly and stretched his arm at Pilcher.

"There's the man o' blood, cap'n!" he shrilled forth. "Flung his knife, he did, and murdered poor Simon Blake, as godly a man as ever walked —"

"After Blake tried to stave in my head, eh?" said Low, pale with fury. "After he'd murdered poor chips, eh?"

"It was an accident!" cried out the man. "I seen his lanyard break and —"

"You lie," said I angrily. "I saw him fling the bucket. You liar, go and join those four scoundrels and take a dozen yourself for your lies!"

"Approved," added Ned Low curtly. "Bind these five men, you dogs, and do it swift! Where's the gunner?"

"Here I be, sir."

Gunner Basil came to the front. He gave an order, and for a moment I thought there would be open mutiny. Then as John Russel grinned and lifted pistol the men obeyed. The five about the mast were bound.

"Now, men," said Low sternly. "I want an explanation of this. Pick your spokesman and send him aft to me as soon as the lashing is over."

He turned and walked aft. Then came Polly Langton running, and joined Pilcher, who was holding the head of poor old Humphrey Stave in his arms, tears coursing down his savage brown cheeks. Humphrey blinked up out of the blood, and saw the girl there, white and feared.

"Oh minny, minny!" cried the dying man. "Here's your lad Humphrey coom home again! Oh, minny, I ha' cried for 'ee! Home from sea, minny, wi' presents for 'ee —"

His head sagged over, and that was all save that Pilcher broke into a storm of sobbing and wild cursing grief. Then the girl's voice thrust in.

"What — what is all this?"

She saw the five men being led aft to the main.

"What have those men done? I heard shots —"

"Murder and mutiny, lass," said John Russel, smirking at her. "But for George Roberts here they had murdered Ned Low and taken the ship."

"Aye, and they killed poor old Humphrey," I added. "Bose, go and do your duty, man."

Tears unwiped, Pilcher leaped up and ran aft for his lash. White-faced, the girl stared about, saw the five being triced up and knew the purpose of it. I called to the other men about us, and at my order they laid out old Humphrey and Ezra Blake. Simon was gone into the deep already. The other man whom I had shot was but wounded across the scalp.

"Take charge here, John," I said to Russel. "I must see to a matter below."

I went aft, passing Ned Low, who stood white and stern at the rail of the quarterdeck, his eyes glittering fiercely. How far this mutiny extended we could not tell, of course; whether all the crew were in it, or only the two Blakes. Perhaps indeed Simon Blake had merely seized the chance to kill the captain without premeditation.

Going below, I looked along the ladder for that knife which had so narrowly missed my head. The knife was gone, and I swore roundly to myself over the fact. Either Gunner Basil or Russel had flung it, I felt convinced, and I suspected the former. As I looked, Dickon the cabinboy came sleepily to the foot of the ladder, rubbing his eyes.

"What be the fuss, sir?" he asked. "I was asleep down yonder —"

"Get up and see," I responded. "And let the flogging of better men keep you from evil courses, younker! Up with you."

He went to the deck above, and I after him. And there I saw a thing that was bad for discipline.

Pilcher had begun laying on the lash, and the first man under his whip was bloody, for the bosun was in savage mind. But Polly Langton had stopped him and now was standing by, looking aft at Ned Low and demanding that the men be given fair trial. Poor lass! She little dreamed what her intervention was going to mean in the end!

"Dear girl," replied Ned softly enough, yet with steel in his voice, "these men ha' tried to murder me and take the ship. They ha' done murder already. They're getting off light with two dozen, lass. Stand aside, and interfere not!"

"I'll not have it!" she stormed back at him. "You bloody-minded pirates, this is past endurance! These poor men —"

"Bose!"

Now the voice of Ned Low thundered out like a trumpet across the deck.

"Lay on, I bid ye!"

Pilcher shook his earrings, and the cat swung, and the man under it screamed out. At this, Polly Langton turned about, and held out an arm to the men who watched the scene.

"Help me stop it!" she cried wildly enough. "Take the ship from these pirates, these murderous brutes — come, men! Stand by me; don't let your comrades be lashed like dogs —"

Well, the words died on her lips as she saw the uselessness of it. John Russel, all again until his teeth flashed white in the sun, stood to one side, and the hearts of the men sickened in them under his look. So Polly knew that her plea was futile, and with a little groan that hurt my soul she turned again to Ned Low.

"Well do they call you Bloody Ned!" she said in a slow and deliberate voice that carried far. "Never dare to speak to me again, you or your friends — I wash my hands of you and your filthy gold and all your doings! Go on; do your worst to these helpless men, but never speak to me, I command you!"

With this she bent her head and, tears on her cheeks,

went aft and so below. While Bosun Pilcher, tears likewise on his own cheeks but from different cause, brought down the cat with all his brawn in the blow, so that the hurt man screamed again.

Presently it was done, Gunner Basil standing by and counting the blows to each man. Then, the groaning dogs staggering forward, Ned Low summoned the spokesman from the other men. All this while Thomas Winder had stuck to the wheel, wagging his long face vacantly but keeping the ship close to her course.

The spokesman came aft. A young, hard-faced fellow he was, by name David Spry, and he poured forth a long and whining plea, full of pious sentiments. The gist of it was that none of the men had intended mutiny; that they believed Bosun Pilcher had murdered Simon Blake and had so acted; that they were repentant and heartily sorry for their misdoing, and humbly begged forgiveness. All in all it was a moving and earnest plea, full of arrant hypocrisy and a lie from start to finish. Ned Low told the man as much.

"What's got into you godly rogues I don't know," he concluded. "But I know who's master o' this ship, and you'll know it, every man of you! Go for'ard. All hands stand by to bury the dead at two bells in the next watch. That's all."

David Spry went forward, and we shifted the men about so that the watches were again balanced. But Bosun Pilcher sat up in the forechains and cried like a baby over the passing of old Humphrey.

That evening after the dead were gone and it was again my watch Ned Low came up to me as I was having the lights filled and placed. We were alone upon the quarterdeck save for the man at the helm, and we were out of hearing.

"George," said Low quietly, "what the hell can I do with her? She won't join us at mess, won't so much as speak to any of us aft. Her attitude has already had an effect on the men. Damn me, I can't take the girl by the neck and throttle her!"

"If you did, Ned —" and I checked myself.

A low laugh came from him.

"Oh, aye! You'd be at my throat. Well, lad, much joy to you of the vixen if you win her. An honest lass, with the courage of her convictions — but oh, good Lord!"

The words came from him in a groan.

"Five years ago this night I was a man in hell, George. Look ye, now! I'm suspicious of this Gunner Basil. Philip, the cook, came to me tonight, and, says he, Basil and our halfwit Winter met outside the galley, and Winter drew a knife on the gunner, cursing him most vile.

"'Now see what you've done, you bastard!' says Winter. For tuppence I'd cut the rotten heart out of you for not waiting, you dog, you!'

"That's strange talk for the daft man, George. And the cook says that Gunner Basil was in mortal fear. This Winter may be harmless, but like most daft men he may have dangerous spells."

"I don't doubt it," I answered and told him of that day when I had come on Thomas Winter down in the cabin. "Excitement seems to send the poor madman's wits flying. But what's all this got to do with five years ago tonight, Ned?"

"I don't know," said he shortly enough.

For a moment he laid his arm across my shoulders.

"Oh, lad," he said softly, "don't you see that the lass is raising hell with those honest fools up for'ard — and herself all honest, too?"

"Aye," I told him. "But how to prevent it?"

"Ask the stars, George," and he drew away with a laugh.

"Damn me if I know! Good night."

CHAPTER III

All this while I had not seen a great deal of John Russel. The little we saw of each other, however, intensified the feelings that had arisen between us that morning on the quay below London Bridge. I heartily detested his smooth, sneering ways, and I think he was unable to puzzle me out — had not the honesty to take me for what I was, yet could not quite fathom me for a knave like himself. Ned Low, I felt certain, distrusted the man on general principles.

Fools that we were! We might better have directed our suspicions elsewhere, had we known it — but how were we to know it? Thus moves life itself, toward some vain objective, only to find itself suddenly directed toward othersome. For now, looking back at it all, I really believe that Russel was square enough in his intent toward the rest of us; but our mutual dislike ripened into distrust, and the distrust rotted into maggots of hatred, all quickly and suddenly.

It happened one day when the wind was fitful and changing, and the air heavy with brooding storm, so that all hands were kept bracing about the yards and men's tempers were apt to fly out at nothing. Not that I make any excuse of this for my own part, since through several days Russel and I had been approaching a crisis.

This came about in some degree through the attitude of Polly Langton. Ever since that day Humphrey Stave was slain she had kept to her word and held no intercourse with any of us aft. Her meals were served in her own tiny box of a cabin, and she treated us with a stony silence as if we did not exist. When she walked the deck, it was forward; and often she talked with the men, and sometimes would relent a little when I saluted her, though she spoke not.

Because I perceived that she thus softened a little toward me, her manner irked me not at all; but John Russel it infuriated, I observed that after some meeting with her he would walk the decks like a devil incarnate, raging among the men; and once he beat David Spry so furiously with a belaying-pin that the seaman bore the marks of it a fortnight.

Not that he had cause, either. The men were tamed, were obedient and lively and had given no further sign of any trouble.

Between me and John Russel, however, the hot tropic sun quickened ill-feeling. On the morning in question we had a sharp exchange of words when watches were changed. Having lost three men, we were short in each watch; added to which, one of the men was ill with the ague, passing from a quotidian into a tertian, and being too weak to move. So Russel desired to shift Bosun Pilcher out of my watch into his own, which offer I very bluntly refused. We nearly came to blows over it, yet did not.

At eight bells in the afternoon I turned over the deck to him and went below at once to get some sleep; storm was brewing and the heaviness of the air had given me a headache. As I came below I met Dickon in the passage and ordered him to fetch me a mug of ale into the main cabin. There I sat down to the table to pick our course on the chart, as we were getting close to the islands and had need of care.

Hearing someone enter, I spoke over my shoulder without looking up, thinking it Dickon.

"We're past the Canaries, and I would we had some of that wine aboard! Go you and tell Philip to get a fresh butt brought up for'ard, for the water in that is foul, and to have it well lashed in place at once."

"Damn your impudence!" said the voice of Russel. "Run your own errands, you cursed Virginian."

I turned to see Russel at the cupboard, pouring a cup of wine.

"Hark 'ee, Russel or Lopez," I told him, "a little more civility, if you please! I took you for Dickon —"

"The devil sink you and your takings!" he broke in with a sudden access of fury, turning at me and snarling like a wolf.

Just then Ned Low came into the cabin, and Russel gulped at his wine. Ned perceived nothing amiss, but came and glanced at the chart and chuckled merrily.

"Ha, good and well done, George! By the Lord Harry, we've a record to boast of this voyage — hardly a ship spoke, not a head wind nor a calm, and a course fair and straight as an arrow to the islands! Gunner's on deck, John? I must speak with him."

He passed out and was gone. Russel looked after him with a dark sneer.

"Aye, you'll speak wi' Gunner Basil once too often!" he growled. "I've warned you against that pale-eyed devil, you poor fool of a gentleman, you —"

"Keep your tongue off Low," I snapped. He whipped out an oath, and I saw murder in his eyes; his hand dived down to the pistol in his belt. At that I was out of the chair and at him and knocked the pistol into the corner.

His fist took me under the ear and smashed me against the wall. As I rose I caught sight of Dickon, ale-mug in hand, standing in the doorway and staring out of his evil eyes. Then Russel was atop of me, and his knife was out; but I met him with a blow from the shoulder that tapped the claret, and got out from the wall. He came on, cursing and letting drive with the knife, but I evaded him and got home another blow. Then sanity began to crowd into my brain.

"Let be, you fool!" I cried out, parrying his stroke. "More of this and well all find ourselves —"

He stopped short in his stride like a man paralyzed, and for an instant I thought that my words had checked him. It was not my words or my fist, however. He stood there with the knife held out toward me, and slowly his fingers loosened, so that it dropped and tinkled on the floor. His eyes widened on me and his mouth opened, but no words came forth.

Then a bubble of red froth broke on his lips; he dropped to his knees and rolled down on the floor, and I saw the haft of a knife sticking out from his back.

Even while I stared at him in blank horror and wonder I caught the shrill voice of that devil's spawn Dickon from the companionway.

"Ahoy, cap'n!" it cried out. "Cap'n Low! The mate ha' killed Mr. Russel, cap'n!"

John Russel, dying, heard that lifting, piercing cry. He heaved upward, raised himself to one elbow, wrenched up his head, and looked at me. A ghastly, twisted smile curled his lips as he slobbered the blood from his pierced lungs. He tried to speak, and could not — then sudden words burst from him.

"Now 'ware of them, Roberts, or you're snared! Tell Low — that the man — man Thomas Winter —"

He strangled in his own life-stream, and died on the word.

Now came Ned Low running, with the imp Dickon pointing and crying at his heels, and behind them Gunner Basil and the bosun. Some of the men were following; but Captain Low sent back an angry shout that checked them and ordered Pilcher back to keep the deck. The bosun obeyed with an ill grace and waved his hand to me before he went. Ned Low came on into the cabin.

"I seen it done, cap'n!" shrilled that little devil Dickon, pointing at me. "Took un in the back, 'e did —"

"You little liar!" I burst forth angrily. "It was you flung that knife —"

I started for him; but Gunner Basil whipped out a pistol at me, and I checked myself. A dying man does not waste words. John Russel had spent his last breath in warning me, and those pale, murderous eyes of the gunner's told me who was back of this snare. I think Gunner Basil would have pistoled me then, had not Ned Low knocked up his weapon.

"What in the devil's name is all this!" he cried out. "Dickon stow your jaw! George, what happened?"

"Why, Russel and I were fighting," I said bluntly. "In the midst of it Dickon there threw a knife and struck Russel in the back. That's all."

"A black lie!" screamed the boy, flying into a fury of rage. "It was you stabbed un as 'e leaned over the table — never give un a chance! And —"

"Do not cast the stain o' murder on the innocent boy, Mr. Roberts!" spoke out Gunner Basil in his best preaching manner. "A sanctified vessel is the lad —"

I plunged at him, but Ned Low caught my arm and flung me back. He turned a cold face to the gunner and ordered him on deck.

"It's your watch, and see that you keep it," he finished. "This is none of your affair. I want no more words from you, mind that!"

Basil looked him in the eye, and dropped his gaze.

"Aye, sir," he said, and departed to the deck meekly.

Ned Low took a step forward, leaned over the body of Russel and pulled forth the knife. He rose up and gave Dickon a keen glance.

"Dickon," he said in a kindly tone, "keep this matter to yourself. You understand?"

The little devil was no more astounded than I was, and could only stare and mumble something about Portugee Lopez. Ned Low nodded thoughtfully.

"True, Dickon. The man was pirate and outlaw. Tell the bosun to bring two hands here and remove the body. And no talking mind."

The imp gave me one exultant, diabolical grin, and departed. No sooner was he gone, however, than Ned Low turned to me, a blaze of eager vehemence in his face.

"George, never mind talking!" he burst out softly. "Forgive me, lad. Don't ye see, the little fiend is not alone? Gunner's with him, and more besides. When the call came cook Philip was just yammering to me about some trouble for'ard, and there's a gale breaking within the hour and the sails to be handed. Let this matter pass for the moment; well make the boy confess his lie later on."

"You're right," I assented. "And, Ned! When Russel died he was trying to tell me something. He heard the boy shouting at you and warned me of a trap. He tried to send you some message about the man Winter but could not get it out."

Low's eyes narrowed speculatively.

"Winter! That proves my point; John had guessed the trouble for'ard — thought the daft man was in it, eh? John was no fool in such things. Well, slip a pistol into your pocket from the locker, George, and take the deck.

"Or, stay! You're weary. Go sleep, and bar your door; there's deviltry afoot somewhere. I'll take this watch. We can't trust Gunner Basil."

I nodded and went to my own cabin. There came a tramp of feet as a number of the men descended the ladder; also I heard Polly Langton's voice and knew that the girl was aroused by the noise. Like a coward I flung myself on my bunk and left Ned Low to do the explaining to the lass.

After perhaps an hour of sleep I wakened as the *King Sagamore* keeled over almost on her beam ends — wakened to the trampling of feet, the shouts of men, the pipe calling all hands. Getting hurriedly on deck, I found that the blow had come.

Except for a rag of sail forward we were stripped to meet it. The first blast of the wind had sent us over; now there was peace for a moment. The ship righted, fell away; and then the main fury of the storm drove down. Through the darkness the huge masses of cloud to windward were lightning-shot, sending an eerie glare across the waters.

Now we beheld it coming — a white line of spray and spindrift, racing down from the horizon under the glare of lightning, I was busy amidships, getting everything lashed down anew, when the keen, cold blast of wind smote us I sang out to all hands to hold on, and we leaped to the lifelines. Then we were smothered under water and spray.

Two of our men must have gone at that minute, for we never afterward saw them.

A poorer ship than the *King Sagamore* would never have risen out of that welter, for she laid over while three heavy seas swept her. Then she began to rise; the scrap of sail forward caught and held; she answered her helm and came before the wind, and we were off.

That night the loss of those two men was felt badly, for every hand was needed; and to add to our troubles the ship was making water, a butt having been loosened somewhere forward and the leak hard to get at. None the less we counted ourselves lucky all told; particularly in this, that the gale was driving us fair on our course, and we might look to raise the islands in two days or less.

Now of the company that had left London, twenty all told besides Polly Langton, we had lost six. Aft, there remained captain, mate and gunner, and we took the bosun into our company as second mate. Forward were Dickon, Philip the cook, Thomas Winter, and seven of the sons of righteousness who were led by David Spry; ten in all. It was by no means a large ship's company, but we could take on a few hands at the islands, for the Cape Verde men are glad to ship.

So night wore into dawn again, and ever we fled south and south with the storm roaring at our heels, the *King Sagamore* picked up and hurled forward with a hissing rush by every mountain-wave. With daybreak the leak began to show so bad that I resolved to take it in hand myself, for it was beneath a timber near the well on the larboard side.

Ordering Thomas Winter down into the hold with a lantern, I followed with David Spry to help me. We got the timber cut away about the trunnel, which remained fast in the plank; the butt had started indeed, and the water shot in the full breadth of the fourteen-inch plank.

When we had somewhat checked the force of the stream with oakum we moused the trunnel, took two clove hitches about it and lashed the trunnel to a bar, just as a port is lashed, I had brought along two rollers, or screws, such as we use in Virginia to roll tobacco hogs-heads; these I screwed fast at each corner of the plank and then lashed them into the bar. All this took time and energy; and, having done most of the work myself, I was half drowned and aching in every muscle of my arms when we finished.

"Now, David Spry," I said, "fetch that calking mallet and drive the oakum tight. Lay more oakum on; and you, Winter, get us a chock of wood. We'll nail battens over that, and I'll guarantee she won't weep."

"Aye, sir," said David Spry, picking the mallet out of the water. "She'll not weep a drop."

Thomas Winter held up the lantern high. I was leaning against a beam for support. In the yellow light that halfwitted face of Winter's altered suddenly to a look of such wild ferocity that I was for the moment para-lyzed.

"She'll not weep, David Spry!" he cried out in a bellowing voice. "Strike, lad!"

The seaman struck — not at the seam, but at me.

The mallet caught me above the ear and drove my head against the oak. So sudden, so unexpected and bitter, was the assault, that before I knew what was happening I was dazed and reeling under the blow. I went down into the knee-deep water, and Spry flung himself on top of me, fetching me another crack that knocked the sense out of me.

So there was I taken like a pole-axed bull.

W hen I wakened again, it was to hear my name called. I found myself lying in darkness, but on dry planks. When I moved there echoed from the blackness a rattle of chains, and I found wrists and ankles in irons. By the surge and heave of the deck, the groanings of beams and the creak of the rudder-irons near by I perceived that I was lying in the lazaret aft, down in the run of the ship.

"George!" came a voice again to me. "George Roberts!"

"Hello, Ned!" I answered. "Is that you?"

"Aye," he replied as his foot touched mine.

"Art hurt?"

"Naught worse than a lump or two over the ear. You're not taken likewise?"

"Taken without a blow, lad!"

His voice was bitter.

"They called me down, said that you needed me — and clapped a tarpaulin over my head as I came. Damn me! That halfwit Winter has the strength o' ten men! Well, here I am, and here you are."

I was slow to speak, stunned by the realization of it. Mutiny at such a moment was madness — or so it seemed.

Whom had they, except Gunner Basil, to manage the ship? And he was no navigator.

"I'd give a thousand pound," said Ned Low, "to know what it was John Russel tried to say about that devil Winter!"

"You don't think that it's he who has taken the ship?" I demanded.

"No, no!"

Ned Low laughed a little.

"This is Polly Langton's doing, George."

CHAPTER LIII

The passage of time was nothing to us as we lay in the pitch darkness amid the powder and the cabin stores. Indeed, we lay there the whole day unheeded, all hands being busy above; but the day seemed like weeks to us.

Ned Low had heard some smattering of talk while he and I were being chained in the lazaret; enough to show him that the mutiny had come about through Polly Langton. He had heard Spry swearing that they would stand by the lass and see us hanged for the pirates we were, which indeed appeared proof positive. Yet she was no navigator, though a good seaman in all else, so how could she hope to bring the ship to any port?

"Ned," I asked during the weary wait, "d'you mind that little black box I brought aboard from Langton? You've never said how it was he had the chart."

"I had left it with him to compare with a paper he had in Franklin's writing," said Ned Low. "Poor Langton! Little he guessed what was up this cruise!"

"Well," I said, "for one, I'm not so sure about Polly's being the chief mutineer. That devilish little wastrel Dickon has more infernal brain than we credited him with. I think now 'twas he tried to get me with his knife that day Humphrey Stave was killed. And Gunner Basil is a bad one for certain, though he may be holding to his pious pose. But where's Bosun Pilcher? He'll not turn against us."

"He was on deck when they nabbed me," came Low's voice. "Aye, he's true, and so is black Philip. But that cursed Thomas Winters! I'd like to know what John Russel had to say about the dog."

"Ned," I said after a long space of silence, "tell me about your chase after this Trunnel Toby. And that day Humphrey Stave was killed, you remember? You said how five years ago that night something had happened. What is it all, Ned? What reason lay behind you and the wine-dark sea?"

"Oh ho! Art quoting Homer to me, eh?"

Ned Low's laugh rang bitter, but ended in a soft word.

"George, sometimes I think the waves are weary with weeping — but pshaw! Five years ago I had everything in life, George; university honors, a home and family, and the promise of a girl I loved."

These words had tumbled out of him as it were; jerkily to the flitting of his thought. Now for a little he was silent and finally spoke. His voice was hoarse, whether from the thirst that we had or from the tumult of his spirit I know not.

"Why, George, that is a lengthy recital, and I am no teller of tales; but since we have a quiet watch below, shall out with the yarn and appease your curiosity —"

"It is no such thing," I broke in. "It is interest and friendliness, and you know it!"

"Aye, and your pardon, lad," he answered and sighed. "I have grown cynical of men, George, and belief comes hard to my lips; but my heart is sound enough and loves you. You've never been in the west country, by Wrexharn and Marchwiel and the Brondeg Hills, and Wat's Dike, along the Welsh country?"

"No nearer than London town," I responded.

"Then take my word for it, no lovelier country may be found, George! My father was a magistrate and a knight, and of latter years had grown wealthy through his shares in the Company of Hudson's Bay. And one day he gave sentence to a poacher for killing a hare. A seaman it was, who had wandered riotously up from Bristol, spending guineas by the way. Guineas gone, the seaman headed for Bristol again, trapping the hedges for meals, and so fell foul of the law and was taken. My father sentenced him to transportation.

"Even the man's name was not known. He was a man with long face, they say, and melancholy eyes and a voice like a roaring wind when he flung out curses; a gold ring fast in his nostrils, and over his heart was tattooed a crimson bleeding heart. That, and the name he went by, was all the picture I could gain of him.

"Well, into jail he was clapped, cursing and swearing bitter vengeance upon my father, who had sentenced him. Two days later came travelers, shipmen going to Bristol, and they heard of the man and viewed him as he lay in jail. They recognized him for one Trunnel Toby, a man famed for foul deeds and piracies. Word of it came to London, and he was sent for to be hanged at Tyburn as a notable example to other pirates.

"So they took him away, chained him like a beast. How he did it I know not, but he slew both his guards and escaped clear away. And on a Sunday night he came, bringing other rogues with him, to Ravenscroft Hall where my father lived."

Now the hoarseness gained upon Ned Low, so that for a little he sat in silence, and I could hear his dry mouth working. I had by this time caught the drift of what was afoot, and guessed whither his tale led. The telling of it would ease his heart, so I kept still and let him go his own gait. He resumed presently, speaking soft and low.

"There was a lass I loved, George, and since my parents were lonely, often she would come to the hall and spend a day or two. She was spending that Sunday so when this foul Trunnel Toby and his mates arrived. They picked their time, knowing that few of the servants would be about.

"Well, they broke in and slew like dogs gone mad in

Summer's heat! They slew and robbed, plundering Ravenscroft as they would ha' plundered any ship on the high seas. Two of the dogs fell under my father's steel ere they pistoled him — Toby himself fired the shot, and that same bullet slew my mother. The dear lass they murdered likewise, and fled with their booty, having horses in waiting.

"And the devils got clear away, George; clear away! They had a ship waiting by Bristol, and Trunnel Toby was captain of her.

"To this I was called home from Oxford. One of the two whom my father slew, lived long enough to tell who and why, and then died. For a fortnight I was like a man out of his wits, and then I fell to work. I raised what money I could, sold off what lands were free and went to London.

"There I bought a stout sloop, armed her and manned her with the scurviest knaves could be picked up. There was a devil in me then, lad; for all I was just turned twenty-one I made those knaves fear me most bitterly. So we put to sea, and since that day I have never lessened in the search for Trunnel Toby.

"A year, and I was captaining my own ship, a fine, fast ship that we took from a French rover off Brazil. They had little ease who sailed with me, I promise you! We were on the Account sure enough, but we molested no innocent trader, George — only hunted up and down the seas whatever ship Trunnel Toby might be in.

"He heard of it, and others heard of it, for I hanged every man that had sailed with him or shared with him. More than once, as I have told you, I came close to him, but the hound was wary. I made the seas so hot for him that men were afraid to ship under him, and he was forced to take lesser berths. Always he fled from me; for he knew why I was after him, although no one else knew the reason, and he was afraid to face me.

"Ah, but he is a man of blood past reckoning! A fiend in human form, George; I've heard how he has dealt with captive men and women, so that your blood would freeze to imagine it.

"And he's no coward, either. Only last year with some small boats he boarded a Portuguese Indiaman in the very harbor o' Funchal, slew every soul aboard her and with the remnants of his men worked her out from under the shore guns, I was there a week later and heard the tale, and tracked him to the African coast.

"Indeed, I found the ship in the Guinea River, up a bit from the English factory at Sierra Leone, and I took her. Every man aboard her I hanged, but Trunnel Toby himself got ashore and fled among the blacks up the river. There I lost him, for I pursued with boats and discovered that he had doubled back to the coast again and escaped me in a ship bound for Virginia with slaves. And since then I have been able to obtain not the slightest trace of him.

"Most like he is in Virginia now. With my share of Franklin's gold I'll buy this ship and start out anew, and I think I'll find him in Virginia, for he's poor and without followers, and even the brethren of the coast are afraid to sail with him for fear I'll trace them down and hang them. And that's the reason behind me, George Roberts."

"You've told it to Polly Langton?" I demanded.

"The Lord forbid!" exclaimed his voice, startled. "I've told it to none save you."

"Then no wonder she deems you a common pirate," I said thoughtfully.

"I forbid you to mention it, George."

"Oh, I'll not! I thank you for the confidence, Ned Low, and if it's ever in my power to aid you, count on me. But for the present — zounds! Here we are chained up like felons, and what's to come of it?"

He made no answer to this. Presently, for all my pondering on that sad story of his and the wreck which had been made of his life, I fell asleep from utter weariness.

It was after night when I wakened, for the trap to the cabin above was open, and David Spry was coming down with a lantern and food and mugs of ale. Ned Low was asleep, and Spry stirred him with his foot until he sat up, then gave us the food and ale and watched us make way with it. His dour, gloomy face was saturnine.

"Wind be falling," he announced, "and we're like to raise the islands tomorrow."

Ned Low glanced up at him.

"You'll raise nothing but the coast of hell, you mutinous dog!"

"Aye, by your guidance."

David Spry grinned, and then sobered. He sat him down on an ale-keg and regarded us while he played with his knife in one hand.

"Harkee, masters! The ship's ours. Mistress Polly be in command of she, and Thomas Winter the cap'n —"

"Winter!" I said, choking on my ale. "Are you mad?"

"Nay, un can navigate right well," said David Spry, and grinned again. "Now, Master Winter bain't a man of God, not he! Nor Gunner Basil neither, for all his pretended repentance; for did we not hear un swearing great oaths? Aye. Nor Bose Pilcher neither. And they all say to hang the two of ye and take the ship. We'll not abide this, masters."

We listened to him in stark amazement. He was in deadly earnest, and we realized that he was speaking for the hands forward no less than for himself. But Pilcher —

"Need not call us mutineers, masters," he went on. "We'm be honest men. You be rogues and scoundrels belike; and for the lady up above we've took the ship over, and save the blood of honest men from your hands. Ye unregenerate sons o' Belial, take shame to yourselves!

We'm be honest British men and sail not wi' murderers and pirates and suchlike."

"Yet you're going to murder us," put in Ned Low.

"Not us, master. Set un ashore, maybe."

The man rose and took our mugs.

"Think o' your sins now, and do 'ee spend the night at prayer. It won't hurt ye none."

He climbed up again through the trap, which he left open, perhaps for convenience. We remained in the darkness. Presently I heard Ned Low chuckle.

"George, sink me if this isn't the richest joke ever perpetrated! Here that lass has taken my own ship from me, Bloody Ned — and is mistress of the ship herself!"

"The joke will end as it began — with death," I said broodingly. "These long-noses have seen through Gunner Basil at last, it appears — that's one good thing! But what d'ye think about Thomas Winter, eh? Who dreamed that the lout could navigate — or is he lying to the others about his ability?"

A whistle broke from Ned Low.

"Damn me, George, I'd give a thousand pound to know what it was John Russel —"

"Make it five thousand," I said, "and Russel might come back from hell to tell you."

He laughed at that.

"I doubt it. So those devils are figuring on hanging us, eh? I'm surprised that the bosun is with 'em,"

"He's not," I said. "I know Pilcher, Ned, and he's a true man. But listen! There's a light above —"

Through the open trap we saw a light in the cabin above. It darted down, a square of radiance, and with the roll of the ship illumined our prison-chamber by flashes, now here, now there. Both Ned Low and I were ironed wrist and ankle, and chains ran from the irons to ringbolts in the deck, so that we had freedom of movement but no liberty. Between us was a small keg of excellent port, laid aboard for cabin use; and I knew we would not die of thirst or suffer from it again.

Now a voice came to us from the cabin. The words we could not catch, although by the tone it was the voice of Gunner Basil. Right after it came the clear, high tones of Polly Langton.

"Nay, I will not! I am weary, I tell you, and shall do no talking until tomorrow. Let the two men lie in peace — look to it, gunner; and you, bosun! If harm comes to them you both hang, I swear it! Time enough tomorrow for a talk."

Pilcher made roaring response, perhaps in order that we might hear.

"But, mistress! The men want to know if you be with 'em or no! It's for your sake we have taken the ship —"

"You and the gunner and that man Winter can talk with me at eight bells in the morning, and not before," came her response, and after this, nothing. Presently the light vanished from above.

A bowl or porringer in which some food had been fetched, remained with us. I took this and set it under the spigot of the keg and drew some port. After drinking I passed it along to Ned Low.

"I have a pipe but no tobacco, Ned —"

"Here's 'bacca and a tinder-box."

Neither of us spoke until I had managed, with some trouble, to get the good brown weed alight and had passed the pipe to Ned Low.

"Did you get the catch in her voice, Ned?" I asked. "And she's sparring for time, d'ye mind! Come, Ned, things are not quite so obvious as we thought. The lass is having hard work of it somehow,"

"Bah! Nothing of the sort," growled he. "The jade has come to realize that neither she nor Winter can navigate, that's all. She's afraid. By morning, George, they'll make us an offer if we'll navigate for 'em. Wait and see!"

I was not so sure about this, and events proved my doubts well founded.

"Who keeps the keys of these irons, Ned?" I asked suddenly.

He laughed harshly.

"The gunner. There's a spare set o' keys in the chart locker, but small use they are to us here."

By the movements of the ship we soon perceived that the sea was going down, but the night wore away intolerably for us, and the thought of being thus chained like slaves for any longer time was past endurance.

We had worse than thoughts to torment us, however — worse even than the rats which scurried about and over us until movement frightened them. It was, I think, with the midnight change of watches when the filtered rays of a tiny iron lantern came about the ladder, and then a sound of maudlin cursing and swearing. Down the ladder tumbled the boy Dickon, by some miracle preserving the lantern unhurt as he fell, and picked himself up with more oaths. He was, to put it bluntly, drunk as a lord.

He set the lantern on the ladder and turned to us, cursing and reviling us with the tongue of an arrant pirate. A vast change had come about in him; he had knotted a red kerchief about his head, wore a shirt looted from my bag and had donned my sea-boots which came nearly to his knees. About his waist were belted pistols, though unloaded, and in his hand he held a deadly little gimlet dirk — a round handled weapon, the blade protruding from the fingers of his clenched fist.

"Pirates, is it?" he maundered, coming toward us. "Sink me, but I ha' been cabinboy to Avery, and this is a poor pack o' thieves and woolsack rogues — there, ye lousy dogs! Wake up and give tongue. An I had my way ye'd walk the plank come sunup; aye, and if the old gunner had his way too!"

With this he fetched me a kick and stood regarding us drunkenly, the devil in his face. Cabinboy with Avery indeed! Avery had died before the young rascal was breeched.

"Stare at me, dogs!" He leered at us as he spoke. "Aye, damn ye for cowardly curs! Silly old Langton never dreamed 'twas all cut and dried, eh? Nor you, called Bloody Ned — I'll blood ye, and a pox take ye —" With this he leaned forward and jabbed that little dirk of his into the calf of Ned's leg. The same instant my foot took him in the waist, all my weight back of it.

"Woof!"

The air burst out of him; he went back head first among the boxes, dropping the dirk as he fell. Groaning, holding his hands to his middle, he rose up; then Ned flung the pewter porringer at him and caught him across the eyes. A howl broke from the imp. Catching up the lantern, he scrambled back whence he had come, and his groans died out overhead.

"Sickened him, and well done too!" said Ned, laughing.

He leaned forward, and with his foot raked in the dirk.

"Here's the first symptom of hope we've had, George — aye, I have it. A good little weapon."

"Did the pup hurt you?"

"A scratch. He'd have murdered us if he'd been let alone. Did ye mark what he said about Langton, George? 'All cut and dried,' quoth he!"

I recalled now how Dickon and Gunner Basil had been thick from the very start. It was clear enough that they had fooled Dennis Langton into shipping them; yet we vainly sought a reason until I recalled the tale Pilcher had told me and laid it before Ned Low with some further details that I had forgotten when I first confronted Basil.

"That must be the right of it, Ned!" I concluded,

"Gunner Basil served under Avery, d'ye mind? And this talk about knowing where Avery's gold was hid — d'you think it's the same gold we're after?"

"It's not," said Ned stoutly, "I was at the taking of this hoard; none but Franklin and I knew where it was hid. It may well be, however, that Avery buried some other gold about the islands, and that the gunner knew of it, Avery's been dead long years. Yet I don't like the smell of it all, George; to me it looks like a plan ready laid. All cut and dried, said he! I'd give a thousand pound if I knew what it was John Russel wanted to say about Winter —"

"Hist, below!" came a sudden low voice.

We fell silent.

"Below, cap'n! Art well?"

"Aye," responded Ned Low. "who's there?"

"Me — Philip! What can I do for you, master?"

Lord, but how my heart leaped at those words! The black cook!

"Get the keys from the chart locker and loose us from the irons!" snapped Ned swiftly.

Hope thrilled in his voice, and I felt eagerness surge through me. Philip was a true man, and —

A curse, a shrill cry, the sound of trampling feet came to us, and the voice of Gunner Basil poured forth furious oaths. He had come upon Philip, had discovered him aft, and now drove him forward with blows and beery revelings; evidently a cask had been broached forward. And so our hopes died even more swiftly than they had arisen. All became silent up above.

"Well," quoth Ned philosophically, "better luck next time, lad! And at least I have the little dirk."

It was small consolation, to me at least.

CHAPTER LIIII

With the morning, suddenly and most terribly, there was laid open before us the whole book of villainy which those above were writing. No, not the whole book either; one page of it was still hidden from us!

David Spry came down to us again, left us food and ale and went his way without saying a word, hurriedly. A little while afterward voices came to us through the trap, which remained open. The first voice which reached us was that of Spry himself.

"I am come to speak for them for'ard," he said, "The bosun is a child o' darkness, and we who be honest men will ha' naught to do with his decisions. I say to your face, Gunner Basil, that we ha' doubt of your regenerate state; and I demand to be heard among ye."

The gunner's whine rose, but with an ugly note to it.

"I accept the burden which be laid upon me; aye, the burden o' doubt and mistrust! For my sins —"

"Stow it," commanded a new voice curtly and with irritated contempt. "Stow it, ye swab! As for you, David Spry, ye are dead right, lad. Aye, sit among us, and welcome."

Light came filtering down to us through the open trap. I stared at Ned Low, and he at me, with open wonder and astonishment. What voice was this? It was new to us; we could not place it. Then even as we stared came the answer to our wondering. Polly Langton's voice floated to us.

"Well, Thomas Winter? Where is the bosun?"

"On deck," returned Winter. "One of us must keep the deck, miss. Will ye sit?"

From Ned Low broke a low ejaculation. Winter, indeed! There was no daft vacancy in this voice; it was the full-throated growl of a seaman, as different from the man's usual tones as day from night. The sickening conviction broke upon me full force.

"Ned, it was a plot from the very start!" I said softly with an oath at my own past blindness. "He and the gunner and Dickon, perhaps others! The man was no halfwit at all."

"We're a trifle late discovering the matter," and Ned Low smiled whimsically.

"Now let us have an understanding once and for all."

Polly Langton spoke up coolly, quiet command in her voice, and I could imagine her level eyes sweeping from man to man.

"You have taken this ship from her officers and owners, claiming to do it on my behalf, but without any orders or bidding of mine. Thus far I have consented to the matter, for the ship was in storm and distress. Now speak out your purposes flatly. What mean you to do?"

There was a moment of silence. Ned Low looked at me and made a grimace; here was a morsel of news indeed! We thought that the lass had been a party to our captivity, but now the matter appeared otherwise. As for me I felt a glow of warmth and joy, since it had been hard for me to lose faith in her.

"Mistress," began Gunner Basil, "it be in the purposes of Providence —"

"Stow it!" commanded Thomas Winter. "David Spry, do ye answer the lady."

There was something grim, something significant, in the way this man spoke to Gunner Basil. I remembered how I had overheard him addressing the gunner formerly in the cabin, and instinctively I began to feel a cold chill at thought of the man. Gunner Basil was no baby, but a murderous scoundrel himself; yet the gunner obviously stood in blank fear of this man Winter, whom we had accounted a daft person! Ned Low must have felt something of the same sense, for he murmured to me:

"Mark, 'tis Winter who gives orders! Winter who captains the ship! Winter who navigates her —"

"Why, mistress," broke in the cold voice of David Spry from the cabin above, "we be honest men — some of us at least. Do 'ee mind how, that day Simon and Ezra Blake were murdered, and men lashed, ye cried to us to stand by 'ee against they pirates and bloody rogues? Well, we ha' done so, and that be all."

"All, you say?" spoke out the girl. "What say you, Winter? And you, gunner?"

"Aye," they answered together.

"And what is your purpose now, David Spry?" she demanded. "Do you know why we sail to the Verde Islands?"

"Aye, mistress," he responded. "We ha' heard talk o' gold. We stand with 'ee, I say, and we be honest men. We want no gold but our pay. We'll not see they pirates do no more robbery an' murder, nor take the ship from 'ee, mistress. We'll ha' no more to do wi' they sons o' Belial an' darkness! Do 'ee say the word now, and we stand with 'ee."

"Oh!" said the girl's voice. "What say you to that, Winter? And you, gunner?"

"Aye," they answered again.

Then her voice leaped out at them.

"Very well. If you be minded to obey me, Winter, go above and take the deck, and send Bosun Pilcher down here."

Ned Low gave me a shove with his foot, and grinned admiringly. I awaited the answer. It came with a scrape of feet, and the heavy tread of Thomas Winter leaving the cabin. Immediately afterward, the girl spoke, but softly, so that we could hardly hear her.

"Gunner, what and who is that man? Since the day we left the Thames, he has been known to all aboard as a man of poor sense, no better than a fool. Now he is lucid, and you obey him, and he navigates the ship!"

"Why, mistress, 'tis the dispensation o' Providence!" replied Gunner Basil in oily tones. "I know him no more than you, but praise be, in the hour o' need he has been lifted up as a horn o' salvation to us! What 'ud we ha' done, else, for a navigator, mistress? If it be not a plain case o' Providence, I know naught!"

Now Pilcher made his appearance evidently, for Polly Langton addressed him bluntly.

"Bose, these other men have declared that they have taken the ship on my behalf, will stand by me and take my orders. What say you?"

"I say now, as I said afore," said Pilcher, "that Cap'n Roberts be no pirate! But as for standing by 'ee, mistress, I say aye to that. What's done is done. I obey."

"Very well; then we are agreed," said the girl. "These are my orders! First, that we complete our voyage and get that for which we have come. Second, that the treasure be divided among those to whom it belongs — me, and Cap'n Low, and Mr. Roberts. Third, that these two gentlemen be kept confined until the division is made, then be given their shares and free passage ashore at the first port we make. Now, lads, speak out! Yes or no?"

"That's fair, mistress," said David Spry. "I agree."

"As righteous men," said Gunner Basil, "we ought to hand they over to the law; but I say aye your orders, mistress. Aye."

"And you, bose?" she asked.

"Aye," said Pilcher.

"Very well. See that it be so done. Who among you elected Winter captain?"

"It was agreement, miss," said David Spry. "He could navigate."

"Very well. It is understood."

The sound of feet and the scrape of chairs told us that the conference was over. I was about to speak when Ned Low, his head cocked on one side, made a gesture of caution. I waited. A moment afterward we caught a soft sound of laughter and the voice of Gunner Basil — shorn of its whine.

"Ha, Dickon! Here's a mug o' wine, ye devil's imp! Now run and tell our cap'n, blast his soul, to step down here and finish the bottle with me. Move, ye damned pup!"

A mocking retort from Dickon, and the boy fled on his errand. I sat motionless and stared at Ned Low. We waited expectantly, and were soon rewarded. Winter's heavy tread jarred the deck, and Gunner Basil greeted him with another laugh and an invitation.

"I ha' no time to drink, ye black dog," responded Winter's suddenly masterful voice. "It went well?"

"Aye," said the gunner. "She's after the gold, right enough."

"Good! Then we'll not have to squeeze the location out of her," said Winter. "Play it fine and slip not, or I'll carve the heart out of your carcass, d'ye mind that?"

"But, lad!" cried the gunner, "When this be done, will ye not run to the other island and pick up that gold I told ye of? The gold that Avery buried, his own share it was! No man alive but me knows the place, now that Cap'n Avery be burnin' in hell! What say?"

"Like enough," answered Winter indifferently as if postponing a matter on which he were none too eager. "But, mind ye, we have to make the rendezvous first, lad! We ha' not enough hands to work ship, and will have less. Obey the lass, mind ye! Let her put her gold aboard afore we act. And take good care o' Cap'n Low now; good care! I'll carry him along of us to the rendezvous. There's yet a fortnight afore the *Rose Pink* can be looked for; so,

Gunner Basil, bide patient. If ye spoil my work I'll spread-eagle ye!"

Now both men apparently left the cabin. I drew a long breath and met the gaze of Ned Low, for the moment wordless. But it seemed as if new life had come into him; as if these staggering disclosures had invigorated and heartened him. All the old reckless gaiety back in his eyes, he gave me a grin of sheer, delighted amusement.

"Ha, George! Now we have the right of it, now we have the whole scheme unfolded, sink me else! Damn me, but the rogues were smart! D'ye see, George, they were stranded in London town most likely or else were waiting for word from their friends. So they shipped aboard us and made a rendezvous with the *Rose Pink* at one o' the islands —"

"Who's ship is she?" I demanded. "Who's this devil Winter, anyhow?"

"Damn me if I can figure it, George! The *Rose Pink* is a right good ship o' twenty-two guns; Spriggs had her, but sold her to a Frenchman before he was taken and hanged. Whose she is now, I know not."

"Perhaps Winter knew all along of our errand," I mused.

"Not so. More likely he and the gunner and Dickon shipped with us, meaning to betray us as a prize to the *Rose Pink*; they did not look for so quick a passage as we made, which explains why a fortnight still lacks to the time appointed. Ye see how they ha' made use of these honest fools for'ard? On the way they learned o' what we were after, and Winter is handling the matter so Polly Langton will uncover the gold for him. Cursed clever rogue, ain't he?"

"Too cursed clever for us, Ned. We'd better acquaint the lass with the truth —"

"Tut, tut! She'd never believe us; it would be taken as a ruse to get clear of our irons, lad. Make no mistake,

George, the devil is loose aboard here! Bose Pilcher knows it. You heard how meek he spoke, assenting to all that was said! Take cue from him, George, and bide patient."

Ned Low was aroused now and no mistake, and I began to see the man of energy, below that gay and almost insouciant exterior. There was a bite to his words. I verily believe he was enjoying himself, was scenting the battle. Perhaps indeed he had some prescience of that which was to come.

"Damn it, I don't intend to stay in this hole a fortnight!" I cried angrily.

"We'll not. Philip will be back when he gets a chance — perhaps when watches are changed and Polly takes the deck. Trust the black man, George!"

"But what the hell can we do even if free?" I demanded. "We've no arms."

Ned Low laughed out at this.

"Ha, George — what'll we do? It'll be a sweet play, I'll warrant you! Mind now, have patience! Leave the business to me."

His tone of confidence irritated me.

"You're damned cocksure about it, Ned. What'll you do then? Out with it!"

"Why, hide honor under necessity, as Falstaff has it!"

He chuckled again.

"When needs must, lad, I can play the pirate very well, I do assure you! Ha' faith, and wait."

"I'm no pirate," I said sulkily, "and sha'n't go on the Account for any man."

He laughed at that, then drew a dismal sigh.

"Heigh ho! Times aren't what they were, George, even in the good old days when Kidd and Avery were in their prime! If we'd lived a few score years ago! What ruffing, bold times they were, eh? Sink me if there's any romance at sea these days! Ships in the new fore-and-aft style, all the galleons rotted out, and the brave bucca-neers degenerated into rascally thieves who'd slit your weasand for a shilling rather than risk a fight for a thou-sand pound!

"Well, a few hours more and Bloody Ned will be walking his own deck again — then hey for villainy! I'll slit weasands my own sweet self, and a kerchief about the head will vastly transform, you, George; should take to earrings, like the bosun."

Realizing that he was only playing on my ill humor, I made no response to this.

The hours dragged past most unbearably, for it was stilling hot down in the lazaret; we both waited impa-tiently for noon to arrive, but it came on leaden wings. At length we heard cries and the stamping of feet on deck, though what had happened we did not learn at once. A little later Dickon came into the cabin and began to ar-range it for the meals of those who were now aft. The little Imp had either forgotten the loss of his dirk or else dared not mention it. Instead of closing the trap, over which he moved the table, he began to shy oaths and hard biscuit down at us. In the midst of this he gave us news.

"A pox on ye, dogs! Tomorrow morning we'll have the hanging of ye," he shrilled most venomously. "We've raised the land, and by night we'll be hook down. Tomor-row we'll string ye up to a merry tune!"

His head vanished from the opening, and we heard Gunner Basil's voice.

"Ha, Dickon! Make no talk of hanging where the lady can hear, ye imp o' Satan! Out with ye now and bear dinner. Here's Pilcher, what's second mate now, to eat wi' me. Ho, Pilcher! Be it true that land yonder be the islands, hey? What says cap'n?"

"Cap'n be ciphering and changing course to make the right island," said Pilcher's voice. "Harkee, gunner! I ha' heard tales of ye afore this, man. Mark, I said no word this morning afore the lass — but I know well enough that you, and the cap'n likewise, aren't no chickens. What's i' the wind, man? Are ye for the Account? If so, here's my hand on it!"

The two men fell into low-pitched talk, little of which we could overhear, until the half convinced tones of Gunner Basil lifted in argument.

"Do 'ee listen, Pilcher! There be an article to which all the company, like all companies on the Account, be sworn; and that is not to force no married man to join us; d'ye see? I ha' heard that you be married, Pilcher, The cap'n might be glad of ye, for you know they coasts o' Virginia, whither we'll be bound; but if ye be joining from fear —"

I listened in no little amusement while Bosun Pilcher swore by teeth and toenails that he was not married, hated women as the devil hates holy water and desired to go upon the Account of his free will. He convinced Gunner Basil too, and only a master-liar could have done that thing, especially as the two men disliked each other.

It was obvious that Pilcher was trying to get into the confidence of the rogues and was stopping at nothing to do it. We heard no more, for the gunner discovered the open trap under the table, and with an oath slammed it shut; but we had caught enough to be of great heart to us.

About an hour afterward the trap was hauled open again. That imp Dickon had secured some rock ballast and now began to heave the lumps of stone at us with many foul curses; he would assuredly have worked us some damage had not Thomas Winter come into the cabin and kicked him out. With Winter was David Spry.

Both of them were in huge glee, and no wonder! For by some miracle, since Ned Low was not at all sure of having run out his easting, the island which had been sighted was no other than St. Vincent itself, the very one for which we were bound. The two men discussed this, from which we learned that before sunset the ship would be anchored, then entered up the log and departed again.

"I'll lay you two to one, George." quoth Ned exultantly, "that they'll go after the gold — take the boats and go — this very night! If they do, we're free."

I would not take his bet, however. Unless we were freed before Polly Langton left the ship I feared that the imp Dickon would pistol us where we lay. And such indeed was his intent, for the lad was bloody-hearted as Winter himself.

CHAPTER IX

Notwithstanding our hopes of the black cook, Philip, we saw nothing of him then, until later in the afternoon, by the stamping and singing above and by the change of motion in the ship, we understood that all hands were at the braces and the *King Sagamore* was beyond doubt heading up for the harbor.

"They'll pick the northeast haven, that being closest to the treasure," said Ned Low coolly. "Is it rocky about there, George?"

"No; all sand-hills, and two long spits of sand protect the cove," I told him. "Indeed they might go across the end of the island to get the gold, since it cannot be over a mile and a half or two —"

"Not they!" And Ned laughed heartily. "They'll row ten mile to avoid walking one. Wait and see!"

"If Philip uses that woolly head of his," I observed, "he'll come aft, get the keys, and free us the minute the anchor goes down. All hands will be busy up above."

The anchor did not go down in a hurry, however, for the ship tacked about more than once before she was in shape to make the entrance to the bight. Gradually she came to an even keel, we could hear the thunderous roar of Thomas Winter as he bellowed orders, and presently we were at rest.

Our voyage was done.

Almost at once we were aware of a soft-footed scurrying up above in the cabin. I was minded to call out, but Ned Low restrained me; excitement was upon both of us at thought of Philip there, getting the keys and coming down to let us free.

Philip it was, but in mighty fear, since he had no legitimate business aft. We heard a sudden ejaculation burst from him; then like a blow the voice of David Spry reached down to us.

"What be doin' here, ye black man? Ha, in the cap'n's chests —"

A cry broke from Philip, then the furious thud of a blow. Spry uttered a shout, which must have passed unheard on deck. The two men now began fighting across the cabin, and in the midst of this something fell between me and Ned Low, tinkling on the boards.

"The keys!" cried Ned eagerly. "Grab them, George —"

I found them and closed my fist on the precious things.

Up above the two struggling men came to the deck with a crash, and their legs showed in the opening of the trap. From Philip a choked cry of despair and fear rang out; a moment they lay fighting there at the opening, then came gradually through, and at length fell precipitately, crashing down atop of us headlong.

I saved them from broken necks, but at the cost of being knocked well-nigh senseless. When I had writhed clear, so far as the length of my chains permitted, I saw David Spry kneeling on the chest of the black and whipping out his sheath-knife.

"Enough o' that, Spry!" commanded Ned Low.

Spry looked about and found that gimlet-dirk at his back. He was paralyzed.

"Drop the knife, now! George, George, throttle him, lad!"

Even as the fellow raised a wild yell in his throat, I lunged forward and got him with both hands, dragging him to the deck with me. Now he was beyond reach of the dirk, and knew it, fighting furiously to get at me; while black Philip, twisting to his knees, added his strength to mine.

With never a sound out of him, David Spry fought on until he was black in the face as Philip and then suddenly collapsed.

"Quick, George! Give Philip the keys. Now, cook, loose my wrists, then get back up to the cabin and make all straight, and get for'ard," commanded Ned swiftly. "Look alive, lad; look alive! Not a minute to lose. We'll take care of all here."

Under the spur of his tongue Philip fumbled about for the keys, where they had dropped out of my hand. Panting like a blown horse, he found them and worked at the ironed wrists of Ned Low until a sharp word broke from the latter.

"Done! Enough, lad — up with ye! Leave all to us. Wait for word from us. Quick now!"

Obeying in his blind fashion, Philip leaped for the ladder, planted a final kick in the ribs of the senseless seaman and made the best of his way above.

When he had freed his ankles Ned Low knelt before me and worked on my irons with the keys. Blessed relief! In another moment my wrists were free, and I was rubbing at the torn skin, while Ned freed my ankles likewise.

"Now," I said grimly, "there'll be a reckoning alow and aloft —"

"Softly, softly!" said Ned, and laughed quietly in his throat. "First give me a hand with this godly rogue — thus! Good. Now strip the shirt from him and truss that jaw of his all shipshape."

In no long time we had Spry ironed in Ned Low's place, and so well gagged that nothing but a stifled moan could come from him. He would not soon recover his senses, however.

"Give us a sneaker of that port, lad," said Ned, handing me the bent pewter bowl. "Aye, a good one! Now look 'ee, George, be not hasty to wrath, as Master Spry might say. They'll not miss this rascal, what with the excitement and all. They'll leave an anchor-watch and turn in all hands soon enough."

A few swallows of wine made us both sense our freedom more acutely.

"You'll try and take the ship tonight then?" I asked.

Ned Low grinned. He was getting my pipe alight, and had trouble with the tinder; but at length he got it drawing, and shook his head.

"Not a bit of it, George! Mind now! We have the run of the ship here below, if we want it. We've all the cabin stores here to hand. Let's eat, drink and be merry, lad! Let's have a sound night's sleep, keeping alternate watch lest anyone comes down, and be ready for the morrow.

"Figure it out for yourself," he went on with an eager earnestness. "They'll take the longboat to row around the point o' the island after that gold, and they'll go at the break o' day. Who'll go? Polly, for one; Thomas Winter, for another. Winter will take the six honest lads from up for'ard to row the boat. He'll leave Gunner Basil here to keep the ship with Pilcher. Take the ship while he's gone, George, and when he comes back we'll have the dog at our mercy! Eh?"

There was sense to this; I was forced to admit it, though somewhat against my will, for further waiting was both dangerous and irksome.

"If things go as you expect," I said, "that's the best plan. Agreed! Then let's get some food broken out before the light fails. Lord, but it's great to be free to stretch again! What if Dickon comes down here, Ned?"

"Clap him in irons."

Ned Low grinned.

"I'll hang that little bastard, George! I'd sooner fling him overboard, but he'd not drown, mark me! Well, I'll not hang him either, for he's only a lad. Wait and see, George; the rascal may yet hang himself."

"And so save Jack Ketch a job," I said. "All right, Ned! I agree. Now to dine."

We were not disturbed again all that evening, for it appeared that owing to the heat and the calm of the bay dinner was served on deck. We ate our fill, luxuriated in our freedom and let our captive snore. From the silence above, all hands were sleeping.

Ned Low had curled up and gone to sleep, and I, on watch, was beginning to nod, when a slight noise sounded above, and then came the voice of Polly Langton softly.

"Are you there, Mr. Low — Mr. Roberts?"

I touched Low's face, and he sat up.

"Aye, mistress!" I responded. "And we are like to stay here a while, thanks to you!"

"Oh, you must not — you don't understand!"

There was a break in her voice.

"If I had done anything else they would not have obeyed me! Don't you see, I had to act as I have done, in order to keep where I am? When we get back with the treasure, I shall have you released at once, and then —"

"You've been badly fooled, Miss Polly!" I spoke out, throwing off Ned's warning hand. "Winter and the gunner have a rendezvous at one of the islands with a pirate ship; they are using you to get the gold, then they mean to take this ship and join their comrades. Go with them and bring back the gold, and trust all to us. Make them take the bosun with you, and do you have a talk with Pilcher, for he knows the whole game. He can give you proof enough of everything. But be careful! Don't let Winter suspect that you know —"

"Ah — I hear someone — I dare not stay!"

She was gone again, and what effect my words had upon her we could not tell. Although we listened for a while we could hear nothing. Finally Ned Low whispered to me.

"Why the hell did you tell her to take Pilcher?"

"We don't need him," I responded. "She may."

"True enough," mused Ned Low. "Sink me if I don't believe her, George! Aye. She's handled things well enough, all considered. She's none of your patched and powdered fools who cry, 'La, la!' and fly into hysterics at the sight o' blood; but an honest Devon lass, with hard good sense and sober wits. George, I take back all my harsh words and thoughts about her!"

"Then go to sleep again," I bade him. He obeyed, laughing softly to himself.

The remainder of the night passed quietly. David Spry came to himself and tried to shake off his irons, but soon relapsed into immobility. The more I thought about Polly Langton's words to us the more I admired the girl's good sense in acting just as she had done. I could see now, in the light of those few sentences from her lips, that she had done the best possible thing for all of us.

She had of course played into Winter's hand without knowing it. Those poor "honest fools" up forward, panicky over being led astray by bloody pirates and murderers — as they considered me and Ned — had undoubtedly been prodded and urged all along, ever since we weighed anchor, by Winter and the gunner; in dealing with those fanatics the girl had been walking in slippery places and was aware of it. So all in all I felt greatly heartened by her few words; and when I waked Ned and laid myself down to sleep it was with the feeling that we owed a large debt to Polly Langton.

Morning came at last. Even before the first break of day, we were roused by the activity overhead. Obviously Winter intended to be off and away with the light, and our only fear was that he would visit us to make sure of our safety. As we later learned, we had been placed in the keeping of David Spry, and all hands were too filled with thoughts of gold to waste worry over what had become of Spry. Even Winter could not be blamed for supposing his prisoners well ironed and stowed; for he, playing a deep and desperate game — deeper even than we yet knew — was that morning on the verge of success, with the gold all but his.

Ned and I broke our fast very pleasantly; and though poor Spry's eyes besought us to have pity on him we dared not loosen his gag, promising to take care of him after a bit. Nor did we have any particular desire to ease his lot, since he had certainly made ours hard enough when he had the mastery.

The stern window of the cabin above was open. We heard the men embark as soon as there was light enough to pilot the boat from the harbor. Water and provisions were placed aboard the boat, and the deep voice of Thomas Winter penetrated to us with his final orders. Then at length silence ensued, and we knew the boat had departed.

"Now, George!"

Ned Low drew a deep breath, and then laughed out gaily.

"The question remains as to how many went along! Be quiet a while, lad. Give 'em a chance to get out o' the harbor. Beshrew me if I don't pistol that cursed Gunner Basil, and we do not want them to hear the shot."

"First get your pistol," I reminded him dryly.

He caught my arm. Steps sounded above, and immediately after, the voice of Gunner Basil himself, evidently addressing that imp Dickon.

"What's that ye want, Dickon lad — wine? Well, well, fill your cursed skin if ye will! Hast deserved it, ye limb o' Satan! Here, pour me a drink likewise; I'll wash my mouth clean o' that damned sanctimonious talk. This time tomorrow, lad, we'll ha' the gold aboard, and hey for the Indies!"

"Here's luck, damn yer eyes!" shrilled the boy's voice.

"Sweet lad!" murmured Ned Low.

Now Dickon vomited a volley of oaths, demanding to know why he had not been taken along with the others.

"The black scum of a cook must go," he swore roundly, "and that dog Pilcher, and they six godly fools from for'ard; eight sons o' dogs at the oars, wi' the cap'n and his lass in the starn — and me left here! Damn their eyes, I hope the damned boat sinks with all hands!"

Gunner Basil fell a-laughing at these oaths and valorous wishes.

"You and me, younker," he responded, "got to stick here idle while they work. Aye, the cap'n knows Gunner Basil can lay a gun! Guzzle away, ye varlet, and I'll go set me a fish-line for'ard. There be mighty fish in these waters."

For a while there was silence. Ned and I conferred together, being in no haste, and were delighted by the news we had gained. Those two were alone on board, which made things so much easier for us. Basil alone was sufficient to guard the ship, and Winter had wanted all the hands possible along to work out the treasure, as well as to row the longboat, which was a heavy craft.

All of a sudden we heard a satanic chuckle from above, and then the head of Dickon appeared in the trap. The boy was half drunk, and I looked up to see a pistol in his hand. Staring down into the darkness, he could for the moment see no details.

"Now, ye dogs!" he shrilled at us in maudlin tones. "Now ye have it, Bloody Ned! I'll bleed the both of ye, blast yer damned souls!"

Ned and I must have realized at the same instant that the little devil was run amuck. We sprang up together, but collided and fell back. He, weaving the pistol about in his unsteady hand, uttered a wild laugh and more curses.

"I'll bleed ye, ye dogs!" he went on. "I'll show ye who's the best pirate aboard this damned ship, damn ye! Take that! And there's more for ye where it come from —" The roar of the pistol, volleying smoke and flame in our very faces, proved his words. Only that collision with Ned had saved my life, for the thing bellowed not a yard above my head. I was already heaving for the ladder again, and this time made it, and was up at the murderous little wretch while he still peered through the smoke.

He uttered a strangled cry and rolled aside, but I was through the trap and had him. And how the drunken rascal fought me! He gouged and bit with the venom of a very fury, until I got hold of his fallen pistol and slashed him over the head with the barrel. That laid him quiet at last, knocking the senses out of him.

I rose, and then found that Ned had not followed me.

"Ned!" I cried. "Ned! You're not hit, lad?"

His head rose through the trap, a grim look in his face.

"The bullet slew David Spry," he said, and came to his feet, looking down at the boy. "Sink me, but I could hang this little murderer —"

"No time," I broke in. "That shot will fetch the gunner, Ned! Get your pistols!"

"Right," he cried, and whirled about.

Even as he started toward the lockers, Gunner Basil came running down the passage with a shout to Dickon. There was nothing else to do; I went for him with the empty pistol, and he stopped short in the doorway, his pale eyes popping at sight of me and Ned. His hand flew to the pistol in his belt, but I was ahead of him, and sent him staggering with one shrewd blow in the face.

He tried to run for it, with me at his heels, and got to the companionway. Then as he started up for the deck I had him by the leg. He drew his pistol and fired down, and the bullet actually nicked my cheek and cut the skin of my shoulder, so that he pulled free of me.

None the less I got him, for I reached the deck only a

step behind him and gripped his shirt, and he whirled at me with knife up. I caught his wrist, and we went to the deck together, while Ned Low seized the pistol I had dropped and waited with butt reversed. His chance came as we rolled into the scuppers, and under the smash Gunner Basil relaxed in my grip.

I rose, panting, and regarded the man. His face was smeared with blood, and though the eyes were closed that yellowy parchment face was evil to see. Ned Low touched my arm.

"Get a coil o' light line for'ard, George. We'll tie up him and the boy."

Breathing heavily, yet mighty rejoiced to be free, I went forward and got the line. There I paused to glance around, and the pause cost us dear in the end. The *King Sagamore* lay in the quiet, landlocked bay with nothing in sight but the long sandspit to seaward and the sand-hills around. We were but a cable-length from the shore.

A sudden shout from Ned Low roused me. I caught sight of Dickon, just riser from the companionway, and Ned leaping at him. The boy ran like a hare, evaded Ned and got to the rail. With one clean plunge he was overboard.

Ned jumped to the fife-rail, caught out two of the teak pins and flung one. It drove within a foot of Dickon's head as he came up and struck out for shore. The little fiend twisted his head and looked up at us.

"I'll bleed ye yet, ye dogs!" he screamed shrilly.

Angered, Ned loosed another pin, but Dickon saw it coming and dived. Escaping it, he came up again and struck out for shore. Then I perceived something else, and flung a shout at him.

"Quick, boy! Sharks astern!"

True enough; a black fin was cleaving the water, and another after it. Dickon redoubled his efforts, and made so great a splashing that he got into the shoal water safe, and a moment later staggered up on the sand. He paused there only to shake his fist at us, then turned about and ran across the sand, and presently was gone over the nearest hill.

Ned Low and I bound Gunner Basil hand and foot, gagged him and lashed him to the foot of the mainmast. The ship was ours again.

"And what about Dickon, Ned?" I demanded.

He shrugged, reading my thought.

"The changes are ten to one, George, that he'll not find Winter and the men. And if he does, what of it? We have the ship."

CHAPTER X

In the course of the day Ned Low and I got David Spry decently buried and reoccupied our own cabins. Likewise we noosed a huge turtle swimming alongside, for the season was just beginning and the island waters were thick with the creatures, and we dined famously.

We laid out loaded muskets and pistols with which to receive Winter when he came, and all the while the pale eyes of Gunner Basil watched us. We left him bound and gagged all day, then fed and watered him and took him below, ironing him where we had lain. He had not a word to say.

It was late in the afternoon when we descried a boat, under sail, coming up the bay. The glass showed it to be one of the island boats, with four black islanders aboard; at sight of us they were fearful, but I stood in the shrouds and signaled them, so that they came on and rowed alongside. I could speak their tongue to some extent, and when they came aboard we had a conference.

They were simple fellows, come hither after turtle. I told them that our men had mutinied and gone off in a boat but would return, and that we wanted a dozen islanders to ship aboard us as far as Lisbon. They were suspicious until I gave them what money we had and told them my name, and that I had visited their island of San Nicholas more than once.

"Your governor knows me," I told them, "also Senhor Gonsalvo, the former governor. They will tell you that I am an honest man of my word. How soon can you get the men here?"

They talked together, and decided to return at once to

San Nicholas, saying that they could be back the day after tomorrow in the morning, barring bad weather. Ned Low made me a sign of delighted assent, and so we agreed upon it. Before sunset the blacks were rowing out of the bay, and so departed.

Although Ned and I kept watch and watch that night, we saw no signs of Winter coming back. Sunrise was at hand, we were getting breakfast in the galley, when Ned stepped to the rail, then called me and ran aft for the glass. Sure enough, there was a blot out between the sandspits.

When we had inspected that blot through the glass we stood staring one at the other in blank amazement. For the tube showed us that this was the longboat indeed, with a figure stooped aft, bailing the water out of her, which we took to be that of Polly Langton; only two others were aboard her, and these at the oars — cook Philip and Bosun Pilcher. They were rowing her slowly and wearily, as men who had been long hours at the task, and the boat was low in the water.

"Stove in, George," said Ned Low, wrinkling up his eyes perplexedly. "Now what's it mean, I wonder? Where's Winter and the other six?"

So slowly did they come on that it was after sunrise when they drew near, and Polly waved to us. The two men were too exhausted to wave, although we caught a faint grin from Philip and saw the bosun nod his head to us as the faces strained upward. The boat was half filled with water, and we saw that she was badly stove in the bows.

In fact, so weary were all three of them that they hardly made any comment upon finding us two alone there and the ship ours. The two men crawled over the rail and sank down, gasping for breath. Polly leaned against the rail and looked at us with a tremulous smile upon her lips. Her hair was fallen about her cheeks, and she was very lovely.

"Where's Winter?" I asked.

She nodded toward the sand-hills.

"Coming. We ha' been rowing most o' the night —"

"Rest then," said Ned. "Come, George! I'll be cook. You bring ale."

I fetched some ale, and Ned produced biscuit and turtle-steak. We asked no questions, but waited, and when she had eaten a little the girl suddenly looked up at us.

"Gentlemen, I ask your pardon, for — for everything," she faltered. "I ha' learned the truth —"

Ned took her hand and smoothed it, looking into her eyes.

"Dear lass," he said gravely, "why speak so? Sure, we owe our lives to your wit and good sense. Had you not taken the head of things —"

Her eyes widened and came to me.

"But — but they used me as a tool!" she said. "Bose Pilcher has told me all, as you told me last night, Mr. Roberts! It is all true about that man Winter —"

"Does he suspect that you know?" I demanded.

"No, no! He was glad enough when I offered to come back in the boat and bail her —"

"Then where's the gold?"

Ned broke out in a laugh.

"Come, lass, forget all else and tell us what's happened?"

"Aye, he has the gold," she said, color coming into her cheeks. "We found it just where the directions said. But in coming ashore we ran on a sunken rock that hurt the boat; to fetch back the gold in her was impossible. So Winter remained to bundle it into canvas and carry it across the headland to the bay here. He was too excited over the gold to protest my departure, and sent Pilcher and cook Philip with me. He is sure that bose has joined in his schemes, you see. He'll be here some time today."

"Good!" cried Ned joyfully. "You, lads, get for'ard

and sleep while you can. First, however, help get the boat hauled in, and I'll go to work on her. Canvas and pitch will make her tight enough to use in a pinch."

When the boat was hauled aboard Pilcher and the cook stumbled off to sleep, and Ned fell to his task, whistling blithely.

I got a spare sail rigged aft for a sun-shelter and remained talking with Polly Langton, who refused to go below. She was much concerned to have matters set right between her and us — but no more anxious on this head than was I myself.

From Pilcher, I discovered, she had gained a very accurate understanding of the whole situation — including her worthy uncle's past history, since the bosun had held back nothing. However it must have shocked her, she was now facing too stern realities to spend much thought on the past.

Now I went over with her the varied details of the voyage, pointing out how this and that had come about; and, having the perspective of distance and an awakened mind, Polly could clearly enough discern the right and wrong of things. Of Ned Low I could say very little, but I told enough to make her see that he was not altogether the bloody pirate he had been named.

In an hour we were talking and laughing together as friendly as ever or perhaps more so, and there came up mention of her native Devon. At that she cried out bitterly:

"Oh, if we could only get away from here before the men come back! I want none of that gold. I would it were all at the bottom of the sea! And I am afraid of Winter. If you had heard and seen him when they brought the gold up out of the hole you'd have thought he was more devil than man! Can't we work the ship out now, at once?"

"It might be done," I said, casting an eye at the bay. "There's a light air off the land — Oh, Ned! Ned!"

Ned Low had finished his work on the boat and came at my call, pipe in one hand and mug of ale in the other. Very merry and laughing he was, too.

"Ned, the lass fears Winter. And I am none so sure that it were wise to lie here all today and tonight. He took a brace of muskets with him, and pistols. What d'ye say to letting the gold go hang, slipping the hawser, and —"

"Not by a good deal!" exclaimed Ned coolly.

He regarded Polly with a smile, his brown face very frank and cheerful to see.

"I don't blame ye, Polly, for wanting to be rid of it all and away from here; but, lass, gold is mighty useful in the world. Once away from the *King Sagamore*, once back in London or Devon or where ye will, a few thousand guineas is a mighty fine thing wherewith to fight the world, the flesh and the devil! If the clergy had each a pocketful o' money there'd be less talk of hell and more of heaven — I'll wager ye never heard a bishop talk of hell now! Nor ever will. We see the world quite different through gold spectacles, lass —"

"A brave dissertation, Ned," I broke in dryly, "but come to the point!"

He pointed overside with his pipe, to where several large black fins were slowly cleaving the water.

"There y'are — come to pick the leavings of our turtle! What better guard could we have against Winter tonight, George? Without a boat he can't reach us, and a musketball or two will do us no harm. So fear not; we are safe from him and all others!

"As for the gold, I mean to have it from him; that's one reason for not leaving. The second is like unto it — I'll not leave him wi' that gold in his paws, d'ye mind? I need the gold, and I'll not see him rewarded with it. Nay, leave him ashore for a day or so without fresh water or food or strong liquor, and hear how the dog'll whine to us! We'll, give him bread for gold, and when the last red round piece is down below I'll slip the cable and set our black island men to the braces and leave Thomas Winter here to think on his sins.

"For your sake, lass," he continued, "I'll not try to hang him, since that might make or lead to trouble. We'll leave him marooned and be content wi' the gold."

Leaving him to argue the matter with Polly, I took his mug and went forward to get some ale. While I was there, Pilcher came yawning on deck. I paused for some talk with him, and he told me what had finally and terribly convinced the girl. Under the jubilant excitement of finding the gold Winter had momentarily flung off his mask, telling the lass that he meant to have her as well as the gold; he had charged Pilcher to watch her closely and to lock her into her cabin on reaching the ship.

What Winter had said to Polly Langton was enough to set any man's blood to boiling. Then and there I changed my mind about leaving the bay.

"Bose, who's this fellow Winter?" I demanded. "He's no riffling jack playing in luck. There must be a name to him that men would know."

"Aye, sir, but I could never come at it."

Pilcher shook his gold earrings.

"Gunner Basil knows him, I be certain; no one else. Where be gunner and Dickon, sir?"

I told him of Dickon's escape.

"Gunner's ironed down below. You must have deceived them all finely, bose! Winter really thought you'd go on the Account with him, eh?"

"Gunner be an old fool," Pilcher grinned at me. "Yet there's murder in the heart of un, mark that! The tales he's poured into me would shiver your soul, Mr. Roberts! If he be not a liar he ha' seen and done such things as 'ud melt a Turk!"

"Go down and talk to him," I suggested. "Perhaps you

can get something out of him about Winter. That man's a pirate, a known man, I'm certain of it."

"Be goin' to hang 'un, sir?"

"Aye. You might get the line and block ready now, too."

I went aft with the ale and informed Ned and Polly bluntly that I was for staying until the men returned. Then Ned Low saw what the bosun was doing at the main and questioned me about it.

"Making ready for Winter," I said. "The man hangs."

"Why so changed?" said Ned, laughing. "Would you jeopardize us all?"

"He insulted the lass here," I said. "Make no more talk about it now."

Polly Langton looked at me, and the color came into her face. We must have looked mighty humorous, for Ned Low began to laugh again and went forward. When he was gone, the little lass spoke softly.

"You must not bear him such ill, Mr. Roberts —"

"No protests if you please!" I told her frankly. "Pilcher told me what was said, and I'll give that rascal what he deserves if it kills me! But it won't. Before we leave here the rogue hangs."

She looked troubled, but made no more mention of the matter.

All this while we were keeping a sharp eye upon the sand-hills, but in vain; and since Winter and the six men could not come near the little bay without being seen, we were safe in taking our ease.

After a little Philip appeared and came aft. We were prompt to thank him for his loyalty, and for those keys which had near cost him his life to obtain. The Negro was delighted with our words of praise, and Ned promised him more substantial reward later, when occasion offered.

I had never seen Ned so full of good spirits as this

morning. Polly began to take all in jest his announced purpose of buying out her share of the ship and going forth once more on the Account, and small wonder; no man ever looked less like a pirate than Ned Low that morning. Even when he stated that he would transship her at Lisbon she thought him joking.

So came noon, and Philip brewed us a mighty stew of green turtle in the regular island style, which we hugely enjoyed. Pilcher had held some conversation with Gunner Basil, but it was all one-sided. He reported that the gunner would utter nothing save oaths, and those unfit for repetition.

We had just lighted our pipes, and cook Philip was clearing away the meal from the shelter aft, when Polly Langton looked up and changed countenance suddenly. I followed her gaze, and came to my feet.

"Stand by, Ned! Here they are."

We stood at the rail, watching the seven bowed men coming over the crest of the sand toward the bay. Seven? No, there was one more following them; eight in all, and the eighth was the cabinboy, Dickon.

CHAPTER XI

Foremost of the eight came Thomas Winter. He and the six men after him had flung away their arms, even to pistols; they bore each of them a rude canvas sack, some on shoulders, others in arms, and by their weariness under that dragging weight of wealth we knew how great was the treasure they had unearthed. Dickon alone carried no burden.

"Dickon has told them his tale — yet they come!" exclaimed Ned Low, watching the scene with frowning perplexity.

We shared his uneasy wonder, all of us. We had expected anything but this open coming. It could not be doubted that Winter now knew we held the ship, and he probably thought the gunner dead; he could have had little hope of Pilcher and the cook having subdued us. Yet he came on openly, the six men behind him, bringing their golden treasure down to the shore of the bay! And all unarmed, too, except for knives.

"I looked for them to attack us tonight somehow," I observed, "but not for such a coming. Watch out for tricks, Ned!"

"Yes, yes!" added Polly earnestly. "Don't let him trick you!"

"Fear not," said Ned Low quietly. "I want but that gold of him, and he can have the island! And let him try his tricks, now that we know him for what he is."

The eight came filing down to the sandy shore of the bay, a scant cable's length from us.

"Way enough, lads'" cried Thomas Winter, dumping his load into the sand. In the hot stillness of the bay, with not a breath stirring aloft, each sound reached us plainly; the hot panting of the men, as one by one they added their burdens to the pile; the oaths and curses of Dickon, toiling in their wake; the dull sound of clinking metal as the pile of gold grew complete. More than one of the godly rogues vented himself of profane words as shoulders and arms were rubbed.

"Gold makes a change, even as I told you, in men," commented Ned Low. "Mark those rascals, George! A day or so ago they were pious, regenerate dogs — and now look at the flame in their faces, the passion in them!"

"More like thirst," commented the girl practically. "The water in the boat's cask was foul. And they have thrown away even the provisions in order to carry the gold."

That was true. The group of men stood there staring at us, and even in the face of Winter we could lead the hopeless despondency of a beaten man. They had neither water, food nor arms. We, who held the ship, held everything.

At length Winter came down to the water's edge and hailed us.

"Ahoy! Pilcher, are you there, bosun?"

"Aye," roared back bose. "Here and with the cap'n, ye damned dog!"

Winter stared at us from his long face.

"I hadn't thought ye'd go back on us, bose," said he, and shook his head. "Be you with 'em too, Miss Polly?"

She would not answer him. Ned Low made laughing response.

"Come aboard, Thomas Winter! Come aboard, with the men. Swim, lads, swim! The ale is warm, but hearty, and here fine fresh turtle, and fish for the taking. Come aboard, lads, and never mind the sharks."

The other men and Dickon were by now sprawled in

the sand in various attitudes of despair. But Thomas Winter stood and stared at us.

"Master Low, ye'd never see us starve an' die o' thirst?" he cried.

"Aye, and with a good heart!" said Ned cheerfully. "There's water to the south end of the island, lads. Take up your gold and go for it."

Sullen curses from the men showed how his words bit, and how they themselves had changed from their former godliness. Ned Low laughed at them.

"Come, come, regenerate hearts!" he derided. "Shall I have up Gunner Basil out of his irons to give you some godly exhortation?"

"Master, we be poor, unlucky men," returned Thomas Winter mournfully. "There be no gettin' around it, you ha' beat us. We ha' throwed the main, and you ha' beat us despite all. Will ye not ha' mercy on us?"

"Not I," said Ned Low blithely. "What about your rendezvous with the *Rose Pink*, Master Winter? Do you still think to pick her up, and carry these good honest lads off to a life o' piracy?"

I watched the men at this, hoping to find that this was news to them; but they clustered about Dickon, merely glared at us. Evidently they had thrown off all restraint. The very sight and touch of the old had corroded their souls. Thomas Winter only wagged his long head and wiped sweat from his brow.

"You ha' beat us," he said again. "We ha' no water, no food, and will die like dogs out here i' the hot sun. Take us board, master, even if it be in irons!"

"Not I," quoth Ned Low, tamping tobacco into his pipe. "I want ye not. You have gold there in plenty. Eat it, drink it! Make a canopy of it to shade yourselves from the sun! We'll be gone from here tomorrow morning, and ye can enjoy the gold to the full."

A sudden transport of rage shook Winter.

"Gizzard and guts! Will ye have no mercy, damn ye?" he roared out.

"Should have thought of that yesterday," I broke in, and he stared at me as if he had never seen me before. "You dog, Winter! I'll see you hanged for what you said to the lass. Mind that! I'll see that the island men know you for pirates, and the first king's ship we speak will come to take you off."

"Master Roberts, you'll never do that?" he returned as if struck aghast by the possibility. "We didn't do no harm to you, sir — only put ye in the bilboes, so to speak, for a day or two. We be main sorry for all we ha' done, masters; aye, we be main sorry! We be naught but poor sailormen, masters. Ye'd not bear malice against us? And now you ha' the ship and all's well, you'd never go off and maroon us here?"

"Aye," said Ned imperturbably. "Like the dogs you are!"

"Do 'ee speak to un for us, mistress!"

Brazenly Winter addressed himself to Polly.

"After all, mistress, we be Englishmen! Maybe we ha' been tempted; aye, it's true enough, the yellow gold tempted us, mistress! But we be not all bad. Do 'ee speak a word to cap'n, and he'll hear it. We'll work ship good and faithful, we will. Aye, he can have us in irons for the mutineers we be, so he don't leave good men here to die o' thirst! Do 'ee speak a word to 'un, do now!"

Polly stood and looked at him, her eyes inflexible. Ned Low laughed again.

"She'll not speak the word, Winter, nor would I listen. Ye'll set no foot on this ship again."

Thomas Winter stood desolate, with head hanging, for a long moment. Then he heaved a great sigh and looked up.

"It be main hard on us, masters!" he said slowly. "Will ye make no terms?"

"Not with you, Winter," answered Ned, who by this time had his pipe alight and stood puffing calmly. "I'll take the men aboard and will hand them over for trial; that's their wages, if they want to come."

"Where be David Spry, cap'n?" spoke out one of the men.

"Dead," I responded. "Murdered by Dickon, there —"

"A foul lie, mates!" screeched young Dickon. "Spry were murdered like poor Mr. Russel — knifed un in the back, Master Roberts did! Don't believe un! It's but to murder us he wants us aboard!"

I disdained to answer this. Among the men there arose a violent altercation. Some were for accepting Ned's terms, anxious to get away from the island at any cost; others called Ned and me bloody murderers and would not allow it. Then one of the men leaped up hotly.

"We all stick or we all go!" he cried out. "Who says stick?"

He and three others voted to stay. Two of the men cried that they would come aboard, and he turned on them angrily.

"No, ye don't!" he cried. "All or none it is. We stick with ee, Winter!"

Ned frowned at this, for I think he had counted on some of the men helping to work ship, and this attitude of theirs rather took him aback. Winter, who had listened to them in silence, now faced us, again and spoke.

"You ha' the whip hand of us, master," he said resignedly. "But if ye will have no pity on us, will ye not barter us even for the gold? Give us biscuit and some rum, and water enough to last until we ha' found the springs, and set a price on it!"

Now I perceived by the light in Ned's eyes that it was for this he had been waiting all the time, for he was intent upon getting that gold aboard. One of the men cried out for shoes, since the sand blistered their bare feet, and another for hats.

"It might be done, lads," rejoined Ned Low, not too eagerly. "Ye have seven bags o' gold there. For the top four of those bags I'll set ashore all the things ye desire; and for the bottom three bags I'll leave the longboat behind when we sail i' the morning. What say ye to that?"

"The boat's stove!" said Winter.

"Aye, but I've patched her, and ye can clap another patch over. What say ye now?"

Winter turned and stepped back to the men. There was a hoarse discussion for and against the offer, since certain of the men had no mind to hand over all the gold. Winter, however, argued with them at length, showing them the hopelessness of their condition.

Polly and I came back under the awning of sail, and Ned joined us.

"Winter has enough sense to know he's beaten," he observed complacently.

"Be careful of him," said Polly slowly. "Be careful! Let the gold go and put to sea now, or he'll play us some trick yet."

"Not he," and Ned chuckled heartily. "Hark to 'em arguing about it! Why, lass, they haven't so much as a pistol among 'em! It'd be a sin and shame to leave all that gold behind; your gold, that your uncle died to leave you his share of, honestly bought; and the gold poor John Russel died for, and his share ours too! Eh, George? Why so solemn?"

"Gold gets paid for," I said. "Oh, I'll be glad o' my share, Ned — but gold gets paid for. Some pays in work and sweat and gets little, like I've done these years at sea; but I've got better things than gold. Some pays in roguery and gets much, and think it the biggest thing in life; but the gold decays on 'em, and they find it's not so big after all."

"Gold don't decay," said Ned briskly, and clapped me on the shoulder. "Ha, George, so art still a philosopher, eh?"

"And I think George has the right of it," said Polly, then blushed red. "I mean Mr. Roberts —"

"Na, nay!" said Ned, laughing. "It's, George and Ned and Polly among us three, lass, why not? Aren't we friends and comrades together? If we be free and easy, it's all in good comradeship."

"What about Dickon?" I demanded. "You'd not take him aboard, even if the men come?"

"No. I had meant to leave him out of the offer," said Ned, and knit his brows, "I want those two men if they'll come; we'll have need of them. We must work the ship around to the south end of the island and take on fresh water, too. We need those men, George. But Dickon stays here, the foul little beast! Gunner Basil we'll take with us —"

"Ahoy, cap'n!" called out the deep voice of Winter.

We went to the rail, and found him ankle deep in water, staring at the ship.

"Agreed, cap'n," he called, "on one condition — that ye let Gunner Basil come free to us. He knows where there be more gold. We can get it i' the boat and join, the *Rose Pink* if we ha' no bad luck. That's our be offer, cap'n, and I ha' sweat makin' the agree to it,"

"Done with you, Winter," said Ned Low promptly. "Now listen well! Those men o' yours shall retire a hundred feet to the top o' that little sand-hill. You wait for us where you are. At the first sign treachery, you'll be shot, and those men with you. Understand that, do you?"

"Aye, sir; but why talk so?" Winter looked astonished. "I be not treacherous, master! It's mortal good o' you, says I, to be so main kind to us — wi' boat and all! Bain't that so, lads? Come, lads, gi' the master three cheers!"

Not they; the six men were again vehemently discussing Winter's offer to them, two begging to be let go aboard the ship, the other four dissenting violently. Dickon took no share in that talk, but sat chewing on a stick to ease his thirst, glowering savagely at the ship.

"You're going to make the barter now Ned?" I asked.

He nodded, beaming gaily.

"Aye, lad! Get the gold aboard and stowed. Then by morning most like all six of those rogues will beg to be took away on my terms. We ha' the sharks for watchdogs, mind ye! It's all safe enough. Wait now, and you'll see; I'll take no chance of that dog tricking me."

Under his assuring confidence, Polly's uneasy look vanished, and I gave over all protest. Indeed, the thought of that gold coming aboard us had a sort of necromancy that bewitched us all with its wizard light.

We turned to in the waist and got the boat into the water. Winter sang out to know when we would release Gunner Basil, and Ned told him in the morning before we sailed; with which Winter had to content himself, taking our word on the matter.

Finding that the boat was well patched ad worthy, we got into her some bags of biscuit and other stores, with rum and a breaker of water and everything that could be useful to the rascals save firearms. Winter anxiously demanded if we would leave the boat in the morning likewise, to which Ned assented.

"Boat and gunner together, Winter! Now get your men up the hill."

Ned turned to us.

"George, you and the bosun take pistols and row the boat ashore, Philip, you stop here at the rail wi' the muskets handy, and let fly if you see anything amiss."

His scheme was safe enough, it appeared. Pilcher and I got down into the boat, put out an par each with pistols at our feet, while Ned sat in the stern with two more pistols, so if need were our pistols could account for six of the rascals. Meantime Dickon and the six men had retired as commanded to the crest of a little sand-hill a hundred feet back from the water.

"Give way!" said Ned, seating himself.

He looked up and waved a hand laughingly.

"Fare you well, Polly! We'll bring you gold when we come again."

"Be careful!" she warned once more.

We headed the boat for the shore and heaved her slowly through the water. Presently her nose scraped, Thomas Winter caught her by the bow, and as Pilcher and I stepped out, gave a tremendous pull that brought her a quarter-length up on the sand.

"Now," said Ned Low, cocking his pistol, "watch yourself, you dog! Take out the stuff and throw in the gold. Pistols, George, and watch him!"

Thomas Winter, his long horse-face adrip with sweat, gave us a reproachful look.

"Can 'ee not see when a man be playin' fair?" he said, and stooped over his task.

Indeed it seemed a bit ridiculous that three of us should wait there with our pistols in hand while one man labored. Winter put his giant strength to work with a will and heaved the stuff ashore until at length he had the boat cleared. Then, wiping his brow, he dropped in the sand for a brief rest.

At this instant we caught a cry from the men on the sand-hill.

"Ho, master! Ho, cap'n! Wilt take me and Jeff aboard?"

"Aye, that we will!" sang out Ned Low, who still sat in the boat's stern.

We heard a cry from Polly. Among the men on the hill arose something of a scuffle. Two of them were trying to break away, the others were restraining them.

Winter paid no heed to this, but lay panting, his eyes closed.

Then the two men got free and began to run, the others hot after them as they leaped down the hillock. The two struck at their pursuers, who followed at their heels, cursing and struggling. Ned Low heaved up his pistol.

"Let 'em go, you rascals!" he cried.

At that Thomas Winter heaved himself up and looked. Then his stentorian voice roared.

"Stand back, ye villains! Back, or I'll break your blasted heads —

The two foremost came running to us, the others still at their heels. Ned hesitated to fire, as did Pilcher and I. From the ship Philip let fly with a musket, the ball going high. A cry broke from one of the men running to us.

"Don't let un stop us, cap'n! We're coming —"

Winter roared at them again, but the rout of men came rushing at us, At a little distance Dickon and the four pursuers paused. The other two came panting up and dropped on their knees beside the boat.

"Wilt take us, cap'n?" they begged together.

"Aye, but you'll stay in irons until we sail," said Ned Low, then looked up at the others. "In with you, lads. You there, stand back! Back!"

Sullenly the others began to obey, while Winter roared at them again. One of the men clambered into the boat — and then went sprawling atop of Ned. The other was up and at me before I realized his intent. Winter whirled and flung himself at Pilcher.

And the others came bursting at us.

CHAPTER XII

I cut a sorry figure in this mishap, for my pistol went off in air, and I was on my face in the sand with two men plunging on me. Ned Low blew out the life of his assailant, but could not get rid of the body before another was on him. As for the bosun he went down like an ox under the fist of Winter and stayed down.

And cook Philip dared not fire for fear of hitting us.

A cruel trap it was, well sprung and full of guile, and we were in truth snared in our own folly. I was bound hand and foot and left lying, but wrenched myself about so that I could see what was happening. All this took place, not as I give it here, but so swiftly that it were hard to realize at once.

Ned Low was struggling both with dead and living, trying to get his other pistol free, in the stern of the boat. She had careened as the load was taken out of her, and now Thomas Winter, an ugly grin showing his fangs, leaned forward and bore down on her with his weight. As she gave, Ned Low and his assailant were tumbled into the water.

"That takes the bite out of his pistol!" quoth Winter. "At him, lads — and alive, mind ye! Any man uses his knife, I'll spread-eagle!"

Why he was so anxious to take Ned alive was by no means clear, and it came very near to costing him all that he had gained. For Ned was on his feet, knife in hand and standing knee-deep in water; twice, with knife and fist, he broke clear of the men and was trying to swim for it to the ship, taking the chance of sharks. He could not get away, however.

At length one of the men got a grip on his knife-arm, and the others piled in. All went down in a turmoil of water and spray, and they haled Ned ashore with a man hanging to either arm, and so bound him.

Winter turned, shot out a long arm and seized Dickon by the shoulder.

"Boy, bide ye here and watch un, and if ye murder un I'll flay the hide off thy back!" he said, in so deadly a voice that the boy shrank back.

Then, loosing Dickon, Winter roared at the men:

"Pile in, lads; pile in! To the ship, afore they lay a gun on us!"

He shoved out the boat and leaped in, the five remaining men after him. There were only two oars in the boat, but with two men to an oar they sent her through the water. From the *King Sagamore* began to bang muskets; both Polly and the black cook were firing from the rail, but quite failed to stop the boat. Two of the men were wounded, and no other damage was done.

A groan broke from Ned Low as the boat swept in under the ship's side and the men began to go up. Dickon, who had picked up one of Pilcher's fallen pistols, echoed the groan in a demoniac chuckle.

Not quite so easily done, however! The first man over the rail went back to feed the sharks, with a ball through him. Winter and the others piled aboard and beat the black cook down; we could hear Winter roaring at them not to kill him, for they would have need of every man to work ship.

Polly had fled to the quarterdeck with a pistol, and now Winter ran at her. She would have killed him then, with luck; but the priming flashed in the pan. Winter tore away the weapon and picked her up and took her below. A moment later he reappeared, having locked her in a cabin.

Upon that, having secured the ship, the men began to

go over her like famished wolves. Gunner Basil was found and let loose. The ale-cask was broached and our turtle was made way with; one and all were so keen for food and drink that they forgot all else.

Dickon stood on the shore and bawled curses at them unheeded. So he turned to the pile of stuff we had brought ashore, broke out some biscuit, opened the rum and the water and began to get himself into a fine condition of drunkenness. Ned and I looked one at the other, but I could not reproach him.

"You were right, George," he said, and swore bitterly.

That was all, but it showed how keen was his self-blame for what had happened.

After a little Dickon came to his feet, staggering, for the rum had shot to an empty stomach and he was drunk. Plucking out his knife, he made his uncertain way to the form of Bosun Pilcher, who lay as Winter had stretched him out. Squatting clown, he began with deliberate dev-iltry to cut the gold earrings from the ears of the bosun.

Naturally enough this treatment revived Pilcher, who sat up cursing. Dickon hiccupped, fell way and retreated. I cried out to Pilcher to kill the young devil and free us, but as bose came to his feet Dickon picked up his pistol and let fly. Pilcher reeled to the shot, and a staining smear of red leaped out across his face; turning around, not knowing what had happened, Pilcher ran for it, Dickon with the second loaded pistol staggered after him and fired again, but missed.

The bosun disappeared over the crest of the sand-hills, whether dying or dead we knew not, and Dickon came back again uttering oaths. A roar of maudlin appro-bation came from the men watching the ship's rail. He shook his fist at them and returned to his rum.

With all these things the afternoon was passing quicker than we knew; but to me and Ned Low, lying there on the open sand, the time dragged like an eternity.

Dickon gave no heed to us, but sat maundering over the pistols, trying to recharge them with futile fingers until his potations and the hot sun sent him fast asleep. The pile of goods we had fetched ashore lay where Winter had flung them. Beyond the pile of canvas-sacked gold lay gray and hideous, at least to my eyes; since for this gold had Polly's liberty and our own lives been bartered. The men aboard ship were still drinking and feasting.

The sun was fast westering when Ned Low turned a white, strained face to me.

"I ha' almost got it, but not quite," he said in a low voice. "When I roll over, see can you put your fingers on the cord." A chorus of drunken song lifted to us as he wrenched about in the sand and got his back to mine. Of Pilcher we had seen nothing. Either the bosun was dead or lying hurt and unconscious like a wounded animal.

Instinctive hope rises in all of us. Now as I fumbled with blind fingers for the cords at Ned's wrists I perceived Dickon asleep in the sunlight of the dying afternoon, saw the pistols at his feet, realized that we might yet have a desperate chance to win. And as the thought came to me I heard the rattle and clatter of men getting into a boat, and turned my eyes to the bay to see the longboat shoved off from the ship and sent toward us by half drunken oarsmen, with Winter in the stern.

"Give way, ye dogs!" came his voice. "Lively does it!"

"No time to lose, lad," said Ned coolly. "I've been all afternoon working 'em loose."

"There y'are then."

I could not see him as I lay, but I heard him curse softly. His hands were too stiff and bloodless for his fingers to work on his bound feet. Meantime the longboat was coming in to the shore, Winter standing in the stern and roaring at his rowers to lay back. Drunk as they were, they brought him in with a rush.

He leaped out of the boat and was at us — just as Ned

Low rose up free. For a long moment the two men looked at each other; behind Winter, the four men tumbled ashore and stood gaping, too fuddled to know what was going on. But I, looking up at Winter, perceived that he seemed cold sober. Behind Ned, Dickon was stirring and staggering to his feet, wakened by the voices. Winter and Ned Low stood motionless, a grin upon the horse-face of Winter, who realized that Ned's feet would scarce bear him as yet.

"Why, here's Bloody Ned the pirate!" said he, and guffawed.

I had never before known, as I knew now upon looking up at him, the indescribable villainy of the man's face; perhaps he had never before let himself go free of restraint. Now, with the mask off, the furious and inhuman cruelty of him was all evident.

"I'll fight 'ee barehanded, Bloody Ned!" he went on. "Dost remember the fight ye had wi' Francis Spriggs on his own quarterdeck, eh?"

Ned started.

"Zounds! How in the devil's name d'ye know of that, Winter?"

"I heard tell on it."

Winter took a step forward, his huge hands clenching and opening again at his sides. His mirth vanished. He showed his yellowed fangs in a snarl, as does a dog to frighten an adversary.

"Fight, ye bruiser! I ha' looked a long while to get my fingers around that windpipe o' thine; gizzard and guts, but I'll tear it out afore I finish ee!"

A spasm of ferocity crossed his face. He lunged forward and dealt a powerful blow with his fist.

Ned avoided it, stumbled a little on his numbed feet, evaded the huge Winter and so came around in front of me. There he faced about and put up his hands, and for a moment I saw the old reckless gaiety in his face.

"Fall to, ye bastard!" he called out — and then drove in a right-hander that rocked Winter's head on his big shoulders.

Now they fell to in all truth, Ned's recklessness vanished; before half a minute was gone he knew that Winter was coming in to tear the throat out of him, literally. After the first few blows all Winter tried to do was to grab with those steel-hook fingers of his. Once he got a grip on Ned's shoulder, and nothing but a full-weight smash on the point of the chin loosened it. And as he came, Winter began to curse.

It was no ordinary cursing, but the foulest outpouring of rottenness that could be spawned in tavern or forecastle. That volley of filth drove Ned white with sheer fury, for there was a venomous madness in it that burned. As for me, I wondered what reason there could be back of it, for Winter's rage was no ordinary battle-anger.

"If you want it, take it, you dog!" panted Ned suddenly.

He opened his arms and let Winter come into a clinch. Both men gasped under the impact, then Winter set himself and made as if he would tear Ned Low asunder.

Instead Ned sent him headlong over the hip in westcountry fashion, and when he rolled over and leaped upright, half of Winter's shirt was torn away. And over his heart there was tattooed a crimson, bleeding heart!

I saw it, and Ned saw it in the same instant.

Ned Low took a step backward, and his face was ashen. For a moment he stood powerless, absolutely paralyzed by the realization of whom he faced. Winter grinned and snarled, and then cursed him anew.

"Aye, it's Trunnel Toby!" he roared out furiously. "Trunnel Toby it be, ye spawn o' hell, who have chased me these five year! And now it be Trunnel Toby a-chasing of you —"

Ned seemed to shiver. Then a frightful cry broke from his lips, and he hurled himself forward, and the other came to meet him. No less was the hatred of the hunted than that of the hunter.

But now Ned Low was as a very flame of fire. Not a word came from his lips, and his face was a gray mask; his arms wrought upon Winter like the rods of an engine, and all the brute power of the other man was helpless before him. It was an awful thing upon which we stared in that moment — a man taking bitter and utter vengeance for such wrongs as few men have suffered.

For Ned Low was taking vengeance in red and running measure. He moved about Winter like a dancing corposant, and left the fiery mark of his fists wherever he touched. Not once could Winter reach him. He drove in without mercy or pity, until Winter was backing helplessly before him, roaring in fury yet unable to fight back. Then Ned began to utter sharp, panting words.

"Take that — for the girl — ye murderer! And that — and that — for the old man — for the two ye killed — wi' one bullet — and that —"

"I'll tear out the throat of ye yet!" roared Winter, even under the blows. "I've saved ye up — till I could hang ye —"

He tried a kick. Ned parried it and drove out with his own booted foot. Winter gave a horrible grunt and doubled up, and Ned smote him full in the face, so that he jerked backward again and fell in the sand. He tried to rise, and could not.

"Up with ye, murderer!" cried Ned, kicking him. "Up, and take —"

Something flew over me, catching the last rays of the dying sunlight in its course; something that curved above me against the sky, like a blue flame. I heard Dickon's wild, shrill cry, and saw Ned Low stagger and throw out his arms. Then he set one hand to his side and pulled out the knife.

Ned plunged to his knees. Even then he tried to reach the figure of Winter, stabbed down at it with the crimsoned knife, but the blade only dabbled the sand. Ned fell to his hands, and then slowly rolled over and lay still.

Then there was a silence. Even Dickon stood aghast before his deed.

Upon that silence broke a storm of oaths and curses and orders from the ship. Gunner Basil stood on the rail, shaking his fist and trying to waken the staring men.

"Aboard with ye! Aboard wi' the gold — aboard!" he yelled frantically. "Aboard, ye drunken fools, afore night comes!"

They awoke, stirred, broke into movement. I could say no word, for the tears that were blinding my eyes, until Dickon came and took the knife from Ned's relaxed hand. Then I cursed him, and cursed him so bitterly that he could not answer me, but ran to the boat.

Me they hove into the stern, and the groaning figure of Winter above me. Then the gold was stowed aboard, and, leaving poor Ned where he lay, they ran out the boat and set her for the ship.

So the day died, and the swift twilight of the tropics merged into night almost by the time I was carried over the rail and flung into the scuppers; and the buckets of sea-water that they flung over the quivering bulk of Winter came running down past me in reddened streams.

CHAPTER XIII

L anterns were lighted above the deck, dimly lighting the planks and coiled ropes and sea gear strewn about. Besides Winter, Gunner Basil and Dickon, there remained four men, two of them wounded; I, who lay bound in the scuppers, and cook Philip, who had been beaten into a mass of bruises and now went groaningly about his work in abject terror. Polly Langton had not appeared on deck, being still locked below.

Winter was a long time in being brought to life, for Ned had near killed him, I lay watching in bitterness of soul. So this man was Trunnel Toby! That explained much — his crafty dissimulation, his plotting, his venomous hatred of Ned Low, his anxiety to take Ned alive. Gunner Basil and he had shipped aboard us, with Dickon, with the twofold intent of pirating us and murdering Ned Low.

And they had won. Despite all, they had won. Pilcher was dead, and Russel, and Ned Low; they had the ship, the treasure — and at thought of Polly Langton down below I kept back a groan.

Gunner Basil brought dry clothes, which Winter donned, his face all puffed and bruised out of shape. Dickon brought him a great flagon of rum, which he gulped down neat. With this to hearten him Winter was soon on his feet and ordering things. Gunner Basil, who knew what arrangements I had made with the black islanders, told him that he might look for a crew in the morning, but Winter was more interested in learning just what had happened ashore. He sent for Dickon, who faced him jauntily at first, but soon changed in demeanor.

"So it was you knifed Bloody Ned!" said Winter heavily. "I have a mind to hang 'ee, lad."

He meant the words, too. Dickon shivered under his baleful stare.

"It was to save your life!" cried the boy. "He had 'ee down —"

An oath burst from Winter.

"Stow yer jaw! I'd ha' broke his cursed neck in another moment, ye swab! Get out o' my sight afore I gut ye! Ho, gunner! Is the boat made fast?"

"Fast, but not hauled up," responded Gunner Basil. "I had thought to go ashore later and turn some turtle —"

"Turtle be damned!" growled Winter.

"Where be the gold? Fetch it here, lads, on the deck Fetch it here, my bullies!"

Dickon slunk into the background, stumbled over me and kicked me savagely, uttering a flood of curses whose malevolence was directed rather at Winter, I thought, than at me.

The roughly sacked gold was brought up and chunked down on the deck. Winter called for a knife and then stooped down — painfully, since he was bruised and sore from head to foot. With the knife he slit the canvas of each sack, and let all the gold come out into a ruddy yellow stream over the planks.

"There y'are!" he roared. "Dickon, more rum! There y'are, lads — fill yer pockets! That's what braw lads gets on the Account — gold! Take it, bullies!"

Though I was across the deck from them, I could see all that took place there beneath the lanterns. Everyone flung forward at the gold. Those four seamen, who a short fortnight previous had been exhorters to righteousness, and honest enough about it too, had now been turned completely to the rightabout. They matched the eager oaths of the gunner and Dickon in the scramble for the gold, until it dawned upon them that there was more gold here than they could well stuff into pockets, so that they all fell to laughing and jesting hideously.

The rum entered into it too, for a keg was brought up and broached, and all hands fell into a wild saturnalia. Each man decked himself to his fancy with plundered stuff from our after cabins; pistols and knives were brought forth and donned; in the midst came a flash and a roar as Dickon's pistol went off and came near to killing one of the men. The answer was a blow, and the two fell to fighting until Winter flung them apart with a bellowing laugh and made each of them down a mug of rum.

I soon saw where this would end. Presently Winter cocked one bunged eye at the main yard, and roared at the gunner.

"Ha, Gunner Basil! Be that block an' tackle rigged to hang me?"

"Aye," hiccupped the gunner, who was reeling. "Master Roberts rigged un."

"Ho, ho!" laughed Winter, and flung a knife across the deck that passed over me and slapped into the bulwark. "Shalt hang at sunrise, Roberts, ye dog! Shalt go to hell to join Bloody Ned, damn ye both! Dickon! Where are ye, Dickon? Go unlock the lass' door and bid her come hither, else I'll come down and fetch her!"

He added a jest to this that fetched a howl of maudlin laughter from the other men. Dickon slipped away aft.

Just here I heard a faint sound, and twisted about to see the black cook Philip come crawling along the rail toward me cautiously. He was in mortal fear, and his teeth were chattering from terror; none the less, he reached up and took from the wood that knife Winter had flung, and then set it to my bound wrists.

"They'll murder us all," he whispered. "Swim for it, master! I'll wait."

Then he went crawling away again into the darkness,

and I realized that my hands were free, and the knife left beside them. That was the act of a brave soul!

So numbed was I that it was some time ere any feeling crept into my fingers, and I was as helpless as if still bound, though my arms could move freely enough. While I lay trying to get some sense of touch into my hands, in order to take the knife and free my ankles, Polly Langton came quietly into the circle of lantern-light, followed by Dickon.

The men gaped at her in shamed silence. Winter was seated on the keg, and met her look with a bold stare. Then he spoke.

"Dickon! Draw rum for the cap'n's lady!"

Dickon moved about the task. As for me, I found the knife with my fingers, and inch by inch moved it in front of me and toward my ankles, fearful lest some eye catch the motion. None did, however, and presently I was parting the hemp that bound me.

Not that this new freedom of mine gave any hope. I lay at the starboard rail of the ship; across from me, near where Winter and the men were grouped, the ropes ran down to the longboat. Gain that boat I could not. All I could do would be to go over the rail and swim for the shore.

Help Polly Langton I could not, unless I attack and kill the whole band of those rogues; and that was an impossibility, even had I firearms. At best she might leap the rail and chance sharks in a swim for the shore. Even then Winter would pursue. And if we got away in the darkness, what remained? A lingering death from thirst and hunger and misery of the hot sun.

I had not forgotten Ned Low, however. As I felt the cords give under the blade, it came to me that I might at least finish Winter, give the lass a fighting chance to reach the shore and perhaps work damage on the other rogues ere they killed me. And this I resolved to do, for I was mad to get a blow at that devil Winter.

My ankles free, I began to rub them cautiously.

Dickon came with the pewter flagon, but Polly took no heed. He shoved it at her, and, grinning, laid his hand on her arm. At that she snatched the flagon and struck it over his head, so that he staggered from the blow and cursed as the rum went over his face. Aye, and his hand went to the knife at his belt, whereat Winter came to life suddenly.

Rising, he swept forward an open-handed blow that knocked Dickon sprawling.

"None o' that, ye spawn of hell!" he roared. "Get up!"

Dickon rose with so black a look that I thought he would let fly at Winter. But the latter only broke into a laugh at the boy's aspect, in which the other men joined.

"Lay hand to the cap'n's lady again, and I'll hang ye!" he said, then turned to the lass with his bold regard. "Gi' me the cup, lass! I'll fill it again for 'ee. Shalt have silks and jewels, diamonds and pearls! Trunnel Toby's lass ye shall be — give it to me!"

She dropped the flagon on the deck.

"Murderers!" she cried out, "Oh, I saw it all from the cabin window! What have ye done with Master Roberts?"

"We be going to hang un at dawn," said Winter, and grinned. "Come, lass, come! What wilt offer for his life, eh?"

"She be soft i' that quarter," spoke up Gunner Basil with a hiccup. "Main soft, I tell 'ee, Toby! Look out she don't knife ye, Toby. Dost remember the Spanish jade that slipped a knife into Cap'n Franklin, hey? Damn my eyes, but she split his weasand! Look out ye don't go the same way, Toby."

Winter laughed — broke into a hearty guffaw. He stooped for the pewter cup, bent it into shape again and held it to the spigot of the keg. When he had downed the rum he wiped his swollen lips and tossed away the flagon.

"Come, lass!" he said in a maudlin jocularity that

might turn at any instant to a raging madness. "Come, lass! Wilt give a kiss to spare thy Roberts a day, eh? A kiss for a day — a day for a kiss, lass! Rot me, the rum ha' got my tongue.

"Bloody Ned be dead, and the bosun dead, and Trunnel Toby's loose. Here be a fine ship, and the *Rose Pink* yonder be waitin' for us, and Trunnel Toby be commodore. Aye! Ye shall be commodore's lady, sweety lass, wi' diamonds an' rubies from the Indies, and fine silk to wear! Come, lass — a day for a kiss!"

No one was watching me; all eyes were on the lass, standing there straight and slim and defiant before the brute who taunted her. I had no skill throwing the knife, or I might have sunk it into him then. I gathered myself together and waited, ready to shout to Polly and leap forward at them.

"I will ha' naught to do with you, ye murderers!" she spoke out bravely. "Aye, and if ye hang Master Roberts I'll never rest until I see each one of you brought to Tyburn Tree and laid there!"

At this, Winter guffawed again.

"Sink me, but I like a lass o' spirit! So ye'll bring me to Tyburn, eh? Well, many another ha' said that, lass. Ned Low said it five year gone, when I pistoled the doddering old rogue who called him son, and when I put my knife into his lass! Aye, and where's Bloody Ned now, tell me? Call him up from hell to help ee, lass! Here, give us a kiss and well leave Roberts' hanging until sunset instead o' sunrise!"

He lunged forward, his hand outstretched to grip the lass.

She drew back a step, then, swift as light, threw her weight into a ringing blow. Her fist took Winter squarely in the mouth, where Ned Low had battered him sorely; and, no less from the pain than from the surprise, sent him staggering and stumbling sidewise until he tripped over a coiled rope and came to hands and knees.

A wild howl of laughter and mirthful oaths surged up from one and all. Winters recovered, swayed on his feet, then uttered a roar of anger. I gathered myself for the leap, and a shout to Polly was upon my very lips — when it was checked.

For the girl took a step backward, staring at the rail. So great was the fright painted in her face, that the men turned to see what she was staring at; and so did Winter. And, over the rail, they saw the face of Ned Low rising.

Terror froze me, no less than them. Ned was dead in the sand, and Bosun Pilcher was dead, yet there rose the head and shoulders of Ned Low, and beside him those of Pilcher, whose earrings glittered yellow in the lantern light. Ghastly and terrible were they, heads and faces streaming with water, and drew themselves over the rail to the deck. From the one side Winter gaped upon them, a frightful honor in his countenance, from the other, the group of men, sitting there paralyzed.

"Back from hell to help the lass, Thomas Winter!" said Ned.

At sound of his voice I ceased to shiver, for that voice of his was alive and no ghost. I rose and stepped forward to join them, but no man heeded me.

A sudden howl, an awful thing to hear, shrilled up from the men. They fell backward, rolled on the deck, stumbled over each other, trying to get away. Pilcher, empty handed like Ned, grinned and started toward them. But Ned Low stepped forward and faced Winter, who was trembling there as he stood.

"Bloody Ned!" he gasped. "Back to hell with 'ee, I'm done with 'ee!"

"You're not done with me till I see ye hung!" shot out Ned, and started forward.

"Ghost or no," rang out a thin, drunken scream, "I'll kill ye over again!"

It was Dickon. He darted out of the shadows, mad with fear and rum, and his arm swung in an arc. I shouted at Ned and, hearing the shout, Ned turned. The knife went past him, singing viciously — and thudded into another mark. The sound of it hitting was plain to all of us.

From Winter broke a furious, gasping shout. He put hand to belt, and a pistol broke the silence with its roar. Then he tired his second pistol. Through the smoke I saw Ned go plunging forward, bringing him down to the deck with raked hands. And through the smoke I saw the boy Dickon, rent and riddled by those bullets, fall across the rail and gasp out his life.

One of the seamen ran at me blindly and struck with his knife, and I loosed at him. We had it hot and thick for a moment, the man stark mad with fear, until the steel went into him and he sank blubbering away. Out of the shadows reeled two figures — Gunner Basil and the bosun, locked breast to breast and fighting like mad. Aye, and there was the black cook, Philip, swinging an empty musket and yelling as he ran after the frightened men. Looking back to Ned, running to help him, I saw him swing an empty pistol and then come to his feet. I had him by the hand, and cried out at the good grip.

"Man, man, I thought you dead there ashore —"

"Zounds, there's not much life left in me!" he said, and laughed out with so gay a note that I wondered. "Had not Dickon's knife spoiled Winter's aim, I'd be gone. But he's taken care of — see that he's bound fast, George —"

He staggered and would have fallen, but that I caught him. There was a bandage about his body, beneath his shirt, and the blood was seeping out afresh from his wound. Polly Langton ran to us, crying and laughing all at once, and as Ned sank down on the deck I turned to her.

"Polly — take care of him, quickly!" I cried. "I must see to things —"

I left her kneeling over him and started forward, wild with easiness to clinch this astounding turn that had flung the ship into our hands again. Bosun Pilcher rose up from the dock before me, a dripping knife in his hand, and I looked down to see Gunner Basil writhing out his life on the planks.

"Quick, bose! Go tie up Winter unless he's hurt to death. I'll see to all for'ard —"

I ran on, and in the bows found the three remaining seamen, partly recovered from their mad panic, roiled in a furious encounter with Philip, who had pursued them there. When I came up and the men knew my voice, they flung down knives and yelled for mercy. I shoved a coil of light line into Philip's hands and told him to bind them

"You shall have what punishment Cap'n Low metes out," I told them. "Stay bound until morning, ye dogs, and if you're not hanged, thank your fortune. Philip, make 'em fast! Then haul each to a gun-carriage and lash 'em there. When you're done, report aft. We must have the ship cleaned up before those islanders come aboard in the morning, else they'll take us for pirates and not ship."

"Aye, sir," sang out Philip with a laugh. I went back aft and found Bosun Pilcher just mounting to the main yard with a line. He grinned cheerfully and paused long enough to tell how he had been scraped by a bullet over the head but not greatly hurt, and how that evening he had found Ned Low crawling over the sand; and the rest was not hard to guess, though I shrank at thought of their swimming out to the ship through those shark infested waters.

And so to where Polly Langton knelt weeping beside Ned, who sat up and caught at my hand with the shadow of his old gay laugh.

"Polly!" I exclaimed. "Why the tears, dear lass? Here

Ned is hurt, but not badly, and the ship and the gold are ours, and yonder goes bose to reeve the line that hang Trunnel Toby — why the tears?"

"That's why, George," she said and laughed through her tears.

THE END

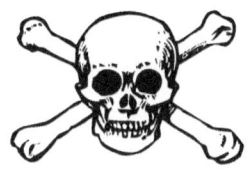

Designed by John Gregory Betancourt.

Body text is in 10 point Rawlinson.
Titles are in Rapscallion.
Decorations are in Fantasy Clipart 2 and Rapscallion.

Another fine book from
Wildside Press, LLC
www.wildsidebooks.com